Deb...

SUNSHINE

**An experience
30 million Americans
shared one night
on television**

"A genuinely lyrical affirmation of life. It literally bursts with the joy and fulfillment of living."

Los Angeles Times

"Immediate experience . . . mind-blowing."

The New York Times

"A poignant story that must rank with the award-winning BRIAN'S SONG."

Chicago Tribune

"Something very special."

Buffalo Evening News

The Story Behind SUNSHINE

A young woman, Jacquelyn M. Helton, died in 1971 of a rare form of cancer, osteogenic sarcoma. The last 18 months of her life she kept a tape-recorded diary as a legacy for her young daughter. Inspired by this remarkable girl's story, and based closely on her diary, Universal Studios produced a stunning motion picture which will be remembered as an outstanding television event of 1973. It received rave reviews, and the New York Times called it "One of the Year's Best Specials." Norma Klein's novel has been written from the actual diary and Carol Sobieski's script of the motion picture.

Universal Studios takes pride in announcing that the story of SUNSHINE will be continued this fall in a series produced by George Eckstein for NBC Television. It will take up the lives of the husband and young daughter where the film ended.

SUNSHINE

A NOVEL BY

Norma Klein

Based on the television production written by CAROL SOBIESKI suggested by the Journal of JACQUELYN M. HELTON.

ORIGINATED BY LAWRENCE SCHILLER, AN ALSKOG, INC. BOOK IN ASSOCIATION WITH THE JENNIFER ELIZABETH HELTON TRUST.

 AVON
PUBLISHERS OF BARD, CAMELOT, DISCUS, EQUINOX AND FLARE BOOKS

SUNSHINE is an original publication of Avon Books.
This work has never before appeared in book form.

AVON BOOKS
A division of
The Hearst Corporation
959 Eighth Avenue
New York, New York 10019

ISBN: 0-380-00049-0

First Avon Printing, July, 1974

AVON TRADEMARK REG. U.S. PAT. OFF. AND
FOREIGN COUNTRIES, REGISTERED TRADEMARK—
MARCA REGISTRADA, HECHO EN CHICAGO, U.S.A.

Printed in the U.S.A.

SUNSHINE

PART ONE

It's funny how you can tell when people are lying to you. Not lying, really, that's not what I mean, I guess. But this doctor, Doctor Thompson—God, I've gone to him four times with this lump on my leg and each time he has some other story. First it was the baby. Jill's six months old now and my figure is pretty much back to normal. I'm skinny usually, but when I had her I did gain a lot of weight. Too much. So he said it was that. He claimed somehow being too fat put a strain on me since this apartment Sam and I are living in has two flights of stairs. He said carrying the baby plus being too fat was what did it.

It's not that. Even I know that. There's only two flights of stairs and Jill's not that heavy. I mean, now she is, but she wasn't back then when he said it. I just get the feeling he doesn't know what's wrong so he makes all this stuff up. Just say you don't know, I want to tell him.

Then, the other time it was the cold climate. Well,

it's cold, sure, but our place is warm enough. No, he said the cold was in my joints and was making me stiff. You just wait till it gets warm, he says. Okay, I'll wait. There's not much else to do, is there? Only the shots he gives me hurt and I don't think they're helping. My leg still hurts. It's silly, I guess, I still hate shots so much. I always did as a kid too. At school they used to make us line up to get our shots and what was worst was the fact that we couldn't go off in a little room and bawl and scream our eyes out. No, we had to stand there right in front of all our friends, with them watching. I hated it!

I've got bursitis, that's what he says. Like arthritis, sort of. But that's something old people get! My Aunt May, she had bursitis, but she was like, sixty something. I'm nineteen. Oh, he doesn't know what he's saying. The trouble is, this town we're in, well, there aren't so many doctors and I didn't want to go to some real expensive one. Where would we get the money? I don't get any alimony from David, I don't want to, either, and Sam—well, he did save some money from the last couple of years when he had all these odd jobs, you know, working at gas stations and stuff. But now, he doesn't want to do that anymore. He wants to try and get a job playing the guitar. That's his real love— Western country music. And he's good, he's really great. I know he'll make it, if he can have a chance.

When I get home, there's Sam sitting on the bed with Weaver. They're practicing their music. I love watching Sam when he plays. He gets this kind of thoughtful tender expression—you can tell just by his face how much he loves it. Weaver—well, he's something else. He's my cousin, and I don't like him that much. He's just kind of sarcastic, the kind who always makes you feel like you've done or said something stupid. That's what Weaver's like. I know he thinks that because of me, Sam doesn't have enough time to practice, that his whole heart and soul isn't in his music. That's not even true, really, but even if it were—love's important too, isn't it? You can't play music all day long. Weaver thinks I'm jealous. I'm not, that's not fair. I have my puss, my little darling, Jill, they can have their darn music.

Whew, Jill's getting kind of heavy, the old, fat, puss face. I get her out of the back yard and start taking off her snowsuit. I love babies in snowsuits with just their round faces with these red, red cheeks peeking out. Like Eskimo babies.

"Hey, that sounds good," I call over to them. "Remind me to hire you when I get rich."

Weaver just goes on playing like I wasn't there. To Sam he says, "The bridges still needs work."

Oh get a girl, Weaver! Know what it's like to be young and in love, you dumbhead! I guess I ought to feel sorry for him. If he weren't so nasty to me, maybe I would.

I go into the kitchen to open some chili for supper. We've been eating simply—chili, hamburgers. I don't mind it. I mean, I like good food too, but this is okay. We have everything else—so we don't have steak. Sometimes I think that if we had everything, that would be too much. We have so much more than most people, anyway. Than most people ever have. I know that, partly I guess, because I was married once and it wasn't good, so I know what good is. I think a lot of people never know. A lot of girls might have stayed with David and thought that was what life was all about, wouldn't ever expect to get more. But I knew there was more. Just kind of by instinct, I knew. I think you have to trust your instinct about those things.

"What was the verdict, baby?" Sam calls in.

"Oh, some old stuff . . . bursitis."

"What'd he give you for it?"

"A shot . . . it hurt."

"I thought last time he gave you a shot and it didn't do any good."

"Yeah, well, this time he says it will do good . . . I can try out for the Olympic track team tomorrow."

"Does this guy know what he's doing?" Sam says. "He keeps giving you these shots—"

I smile. I love teasing Sam. "Well, if you have to know, we're having this thing, see, and we figured you'd never find out if I had to keep going back for my knee."

With a big roar, Sam leaps up from the bed, runs into the kitchen and starts kissing me, hugging me, laughing. He's big and his face scratches. Wow, I love him, he's like a bear.

He makes a sign to Weaver to leave, and Weaver gets this real sour look. "You oughta be a plumber, man, not a musician," he says.

But he leaves. Good riddance, old pal. We roll on the bed, kissing and hugging. Jill is looking at us, puzzled, not knowing what's going on. Sam lifts her up and brings her down on the bed with us. I feel like everything I love is in this bed with me right now, my baby, my guy, and we're all rolled up in the quilt, laughing. Once I saw this statue of a man and a woman and a child but they were all one, all carved together, and that's how I feel when we're all together like this. We're one thing, one person.

I used to think it would matter that Sam wasn't Jill's father. I mean, I thought he couldn't love her the way a real father could. But it's not so. He's so good to her, so patient, so kind. Now he says he would've gone with

me just for her, only when we met, she wasn't even
born yet. But she was in me, she was part of me. I feel
Sam never knew me before Jill. He's always known me
happy. I guess if he'd met me when I was with David,
he wouldn't have thought much of me. I was always in
a rotten mood then, always complaining. Now I feel I
had a right to be. I mean, I think people deserve to be
happy, and if they're not they have a right to feel
cheated. Of course, who said I had to marry him, at
sixteen especially? Yeah, I realize that. It was my
choice and sort of a dumb one. I wanted to get away
from home mostly, that was the main part.

And David's not a monster. He's—well, he's much
straighter than Sam. He went through college and he
was already studying to be a geologist when I met him.
He seemed so grown up to me. All the kids I knew
didn't know which end was up. Maybe that was from
living in a small town—Three Forks—but also they
were young. The guys I knew were so young, they
didn't know anything. David seemed so solid. I was really flattered when he noticed me. And he'd listen when
I talked—I was a real chatterbox then. He'd listen,
like what I said was important and smart. He wasn't a
monster, David. I guess now that I have Sam I don't
resent David so much. I feel like maybe some day he'll
meet the right girl and be happy, only I wasn't the
right girl. He'd never have been happy with me. He
said he was. He said he never could see what I was
complaining about, but I think he did see, he just
didn't want to admit it. He's one of those slow, cautious
people who decides things slowly, but when he does he
hates to admit he was wrong.

You might find it hard to believe this, but David
wouldn't even sleep with me before we got married. He
thought I was too young, what would my parents say.

He's like that—honorable. We had these crazy scenes where I'd be saying—oh let's, why not, we're engaged and all that, and he'd say no, we ought to wait. I guess I liked that in him too, though it seemed a little crazy. I mean, most other guys always seemed to want to, whether they loved you or not, and he really did love me and he wanted to wait. I dug that, I really did.

The thing that got me so mad, more than mad, hurt really, was when I told Mom we were getting married and she said, "You little whore." She was sure I was pregnant! I wasn't! Gosh, I was a virgin, even, and one reason I was was because she'd been screaming at us—there were four of us, all girls—ever since I can remember about how important it was to be a virgin when you got married. And I wanted to please her. I was like a little girl, in that way. Well, I *was* a little girl—just sixteen. Not that eighteen's so old, but now, having been married and with Jill—I feel so much older. Much more than just two and a half years older. Then, I had been living at home all my life, except for this one summer when I ran away, when I was fourteen. And when Mom said that, I just felt so awful. I'd done exactly what she said we should do and it didn't matter, she still didn't trust me or love me. Why?

It's so crazy, but Mom has never really loved me. And I feel like I must have done something bad to make her feel that way. I'd almost rather think it was because I did something bad than to think it just happened, for no good reason. Partly, which is funny, I think I remind her of herself. I look like her, more than the others do. I have long, black hair like hers and hell, I'm pretty. I was always "the pretty one", but pretty like her, kind of sassy and smart. And I think I was like her in being kind of emotional and saying and doing what I felt. Winona—she's my oldest sister—

she's kind of calm and solid, more like Dad's side of the family. She's not married, she lives in New York now and she's studying biology. I loved her the most because she was like a mommy to me, very kind and gentle. Whenever Mom or Dad were mean to me, I'd go to Winona. She didn't always take my side, but she was kind. Even though we were so different. And she loves the land, like me—that was another bond between us, especially as I got older. I guess Mom respected Winona, even though they weren't that close. Winona was so smart, Mom was always a little scared of her.

Darleen is the next one, two years younger than Winona. She's married now with four kids and she lives right near Mom and Dad. Her husband, Joe, works in a hardware store. For some reason, Mom and Darleen always got on like crazy. Almost like two friends at school, whispering and hugging. I felt so left out when they were together. Even now that Darleen is married, she comes to Mom for everything and I mean everything! Mom even goes over there and sets Darleen's hair and helps her tint it this revolting yellow color every week. And they trade recipes, they're into that whole housewife bit. I really wonder sometimes what would happen to Darleen if Mom died or even moved away, not that that's likely in the immediate future. But I think she might just flip out. I guess that makes Mom feel good, feeling so needed. I mean, I needed her too, but I could never show it the same way. If I know someone loves me, like with Sam, I can show it, but I hate that feeling of pleading with someone for love, it's too demeaning.

Pat is the baby, she's younger than me. Maybe I was sort of the middle child. I think Mom had Darleen and Winona and then might have stopped, but Dad really

wanted a boy so they figured they'd keep trying. I
think that's stupid. I'd never, *never* have a baby if I
wasn't going to love it no matter what. And I wouldn't
care what my husband or anyone said. So then I came
along and I guess everyone was real disappointed. And
I was one of those wriggly, fresh little kids that gets
into everything and messes things up—Winona and
Darleen were really neat, both of them. So maybe I
wasn't such a joy to have around. By the time Pat
came, I think Mom didn't care so much. I think she
knew she wasn't going to have a boy and was sort of
reconciled to it. Pat is little and thin and pale—she's always had some kind of sickness since she was born.
Starting when she was three, she had to wear these
glasses, her eyes are really bad, she's almost blind without them. So she was everyone's baby. I love her a lot.
I guess I was mean to her when we were little. I didn't
want her tagging around after me, and I always made
her be the dog or the baby in our games, but I love
her. I felt like I wanted to take care of her and be good
to her—she's like that.

I don't like the night time. It seems like at night all the bad things that happened during the day, all the things I've worried about but pushed away, come creeping back. Not always, just sometimes. This one night I fell asleep and had a nightmare. It was all mixed up, not really clear—my dreams never are—but in it the doctor was telling me something bad about my leg, that I was going to die, and I woke up so scared. It was so real!

Sam is sleeping—he always sleeps like a log. Jill is in her crib, sleeping too. I hate waking Sam up, it doesn't seem fair. But I feel so lonely and scared sitting here, being the only one awake.

Finally, I give him just a little shove and whisper, "Sam?"

He opens his eyes and holds me in his arms, the way I want him to. Oh, I feel better, but worse, too. I'm crying, I knew I would. "He's wrong, Sam," I say. "That doctor ... it's something worse ... I know."

He strokes my head. "Sweetheart . . . don't."

It's so good to be here with him. "Ssh," he says. "Don't wake Jill . . ."

"But I had this dream," I say.

"Dreams don't mean anything."

I want him to be right. Oh, I know, if you asked me in the morning, do dreams mean anything, I'd say no, of course not, don't be silly. But now—it seemed so real. I can almost remember the doctor's face.

Sam goes back to sleep with his arms still around me. He's so loving, so good. Am I too happy? Oh, that's silly, that's superstitious again. I remember when I was little and scared of the dark, I used to go into Mom and Dad's room. They didn't like me to, so I wouldn't even tell them I was there. I'd just creep into their bed at the foot of it and stay there till I felt better. Only once I fell asleep and wet the bed and Dad woke up and got really mad at me.

Jill, I won't do that to you. I'll let you come in my bed whenever you want. I don't care if you wet it. You're scared, that's all, and when babies are scared, they wet their pants. I hate the way Darleen is with her children—just the way Mom was with us, I guess, too strict and setting dumb rules that don't even make sense. I want Jill to be free, the way I wasn't.

She's such a good baby. I miss having her wake up at night and want to nurse. When she was six weeks, she slept right through the night! Such an angel! Just by herself she did it. But I used to like getting up and nursing her. It would be so quiet and I'd bring her into bed with me. I'd prop myself up with a pillow and she'd drink quietly, and Sam would be sleeping there. I never felt scared then, even though it was dark. I just felt really peaceful and good.

I always wanted a baby, especially a baby girl, but I

always wondered too if it would be as good as they say. So many things aren't. So many things they build up in this false romantic way that I hate. So I wondered if maybe having a baby wouldn't be like that. But it was great. Not just having her but nursing her, holding her. I want to nurse her till she's a year. I guess when her teeth start coming in, it might hurt a little, but her teeth aren't in yet, they're slow I guess. Good. Let them be slow.

Wake up, Jill, wake up and comfort me. Let me hold you. No, I can't wake her up just to comfort me, that's selfish. I just look over at her. She sleeps on her stomach. She sucks her thumb when she sleeps, but now it's just outside her mouth, like it popped out in her sleep. Her big round head, her little rump sticking up in the air. Little puss. Don't have bad dreams. But if you do, come to me and I'll hold you. I always will. I'll never say you're too old.

The mountains are beautiful now. It's spring, but now there's still snow, almost blue-white. Sam and I have snowball fights, we horse around. I like it that with Sam I can still be a kid. Sometimes I feel grownup with Jill and all, but sometimes I just want to hack around, to act silly. With David I always felt I had to be serious, sort of, not really myself. He didn't approve of me when I was silly.

Wow, up here I feel so happy I'm going to explode. I'm so full of love for my baby and my man and these absolutely mind blowing mountains, there isn't room for anything else, there isn't room for pain or sickness, or fear. Life's too incredibly beautiful.

I hope so much that when Jill grows up there'll still be places like this she can come to, beautiful places that aren't spoiled. I'm not so much into politics, but the thing I care about most with all that is saving our land. I think that's so important. Maybe it's from having grown up here, out west. Oh, it's changed already, I know. And Dad is always talking about how much nicer it was when he was young—he's from Montana and he used to go hunting and fishing with his dad when he was little. Even so, there are still places like this you can go to, and the worst thing would be if ever they disappeared or got polluted ... I could never go live in a big city like Winona is. Of course, she has to for her studies, but I think I'd hate it. Three Forks was too small, there wasn't that much to do, I always wanted to get away, but I'd never want a place with all concrete and no trees like I imagine New York must be.

It's morning. Sam's out getting some fire wood. He got a pretty good fire going. I can see it out of the corner of my eye as I give Jill a bath. I just bathe her in this iron washtub—it's big enough. I put it on the table so it's steady and can't tip. At home I do her in the kitchen sink, or I used to anyway, she's getting kind of big for that now. Sometimes I like to let her take a bath with me. I just put in a little water, maybe a couple of inches, and I get in first and then I lift her in. She loves it! She has a couple of plastic toys—a frog and a giraffe—and we play with them. Sometimes I get out because I have to, to fix dinner or something, and I wish I could let her stay in. Only they say that's dangerous, she might drown.

She loves her bath, even here in the iron washtub with not much room to move around. I can't let her stay in long, it's too chilly, though near the fire it's not so bad. Her body is so great. She's so round and shiny, and she sits there so squat, like a little Buddha. She seems to love the feeling of me running the sponge over her body. Babies are great that way, when you do something that makes their bodies feel good, they just beam at you. They don't mind showing it, but I think grownups feel self-conscious. I still do, a little. Sometimes Sam wants to make love out of doors when we're alone in the mountains, or with the sun streaming in the window, and it took me a while to get used to it.

I wash her hair with a little baby shampoo. She hasn't got much hair to speak of, it's light, so what there is doesn't show much. That and her being fat seem to make some people think she's a boy. I guess, also, I never like dressing her in light pink the way you're supposed to to let people know what sex a baby is. I always hated pastel colors, especially light pink. I like red and bright yellow and shocking pink, real bright, glowing colors. Anyway, I don't think Jill looks like a boy. It gets me mad sometime. The other day this old couple were admiring her in the store and the man said, "What remarkable eyes he has, very wise. He'll be a great mathematician some day." I just said, "She's a girl" and he said, "Oh . . ." and I thought: so can't she still be a great mathematician anyhow? I mean, she probably wouldn't either way, but it kind of riled me that when I said she was a girl he looked so taken aback, as though saying her eyes looked "wise" couldn't be right. You are wise, aren't you, pooch?

I like to talk to Jill. I know she can't really understand what I'm saying, but she looks at me like she can or, anyway she likes to hear me babbling away. "You think one day you'll have long silky curls? I say, trying to get the soap off her—she's so slippery!—"Then you can be Alice in Wonderland and I'll be the White Rabbit and Daddy'll be the Mad Hatter." She reaches for me, she wants to get out. "Cool it there a minute, hon,"

I say. "You can't get out with all that soap on you or—"

She just wants to get out, the monkey! Look at her, trying to get up, trying to put her arms around me. Oh well, a little soap won't kill her. I reach in back of me for the towel.

Christ! What's happening? Oh my God, I can't stand up, oh Jesus, baby, don't fall, don't let me drop you, oh God, I'm going to. I scream and Sam comes running in. "Get Jill, is she okay?" I yell. "Is she hurt? Get her! Get her!"

"Are *you* all right?" Sam says.

"Get *Jill!*" I scream. I hear her crying. Oh my baby, be okay, please.

Sam goes and picks her up, wraps her in a towel and brings her to me. She's still crying a little, but she quiets down when I hold her and cuddle her. "Little puss, I'm so sorry, are you okay?" Oh, I know she can't talk. Well, she seems okay. I can't see any place she's hurt. Thank God.

"What happened?" Sam says.

"I don't know."

"Did you slip or something? How did you fall?"

I just look at him. We move over to the couch and sit down. "It was my leg . . . it just seemed to—"

"Hurt?"

"Like, collapse. I can't describe it exactly. Like it wasn't there when I went to stand on it."

Sam sits there, looking at my leg. There's still that bump that's been there since November. Sometimes it's hot, like it had a fever. "Listen, we're going back to Riverdale right now, right today. No more of this shit. You're going to a decent doctor, one we'll pay for. No more of this crap with that clinic and that old fogey who doesn't know anything."

He's angry. I can tell by the way he storms out with the washtub and tosses the bath water out the back. I just feel—quiet inside, the way you feel after a thing has happened. When I started falling I was just scared, scared for Jill most of all. Maybe if I hadn't been carrying her, I would have felt the pain more. "Dr. Thompson's okay," I say, sort of under my breath.

"Jesus, come *on*, Kate!"

"You never even met him! How do you know?"

"What's he done but waste our time?"

"He did his best, I guess."

I sit there, watching him throw our stuff together. Jill watches him too. I can feel her getting sleepy as she leans against me. "Listen, I went to the clinic to save us money," I say.

"Sure, great bargain . . . It'll wind up costing ten times what it would've if we'd gone to a real doctor to begin with."

"He *was* real! What do you mean—real? He's an M.D."

"He graduated medical school around nineteen hundred . . . What does he know? . . . Weaver's got this lead on a used bike and now we'll have to use every damn penny on another doctor."

I feel so angry, and so depressed because I think he's right. Why did I keep going when I knew he was no good? Because I didn't want to know? I don't know. "I don't *enjoy* being sick," I say. "I'm not doing it on purpose . . . How do you think I feel, practically killing my baby! Quit blaming me!" I'm almost yelling. Thinking all over again what might have happened to Jill scares me.

"All I'm saying," Sam says, "is that if you'd gone to a decent doctor right from the start, you'd be well by now . . . By waiting six months it's going to take ten times longer to cure. It's going to be ten times as expensive . . . And we can't afford it."

"So, go . . . Nobody says you have to spend your money on me . . . No strings, remember? Just get out."

He says nothing. We just stare at each other.

"What does *that* mean?" he says.

"Leave. Go get your stupid bike . . . I'll cope."

He's watching me. "Will you? . . . Sure, probably you will . . . What am I here for, anyhow? Decoration? Comic relief? . . . Shall I leave? Really?"

I just shrug. "Please yourself."

He takes his guitar, goes into the bedroom and slams the door.

Jill is asleep in my arms. I guess our big scene didn't impress her much. These dumb grownups, yelling their dumb fool heads off, she probably thinks.

Oh Christ, I feel scared. Don't leave, Sam. Not now . . . It's funny. Before I met Sam, I think I could've coped. I had this job, kind of a dinky job in this beauty shop. They couldn't let me set hair or anything, I just swept up and washed peoples' hair and stuff. It was this really funny place because it seemed to be just old ladies. Everyone was, like, around seventy years old. They'd come tottering in, one lady even was wheeled in in a wheelchair just to have her hair set. They hardly had any hair, some of them! Just light little wisps. I felt so sorry for them. I mean, what were they getting all dolled up for? Just to go home and sit in some room all by themselves. Some of them seemed to live with their sisters or sometimes with a husband. Only all the time the sister would be taken sick or the husband would have a heart attack or one of them would have some dizzy spell. Really, there was almost no day when I didn't hear one of those stories. It was kind of morbid, I guess, only at the time I didn't think of it. I felt so good, being pregnant with Jill. I guess I was like in a screen, in my own world, just daydreaming, not really caring too much.

But now I need Sam, I've gotten used to him, I love him. Would I cope? Yeah, I guess. I'd have to. But I'd hate it. I wish I could say that to him, but I can't. Too much pride, I guess. I say it through the slammed door. Don't leave, honey.

Dr. Jack Lincoln is different from Dr. Thompson. Not as old. Sort of solid and graying with glasses. Not so nice. Not mean, just kind of stern and factual. He comes out with the x-rays and shuffles through them. I have the feeling he's stalling for time.

"Well, there seems to be the possibility of cancer here."

It's the first time anyone has said that word, and it freezes me clear though. It's as though I knew he was going to say it, but hearing it is still so much worse than just imagining it. I just stare at him; I can't think what to say.

"I would suggest you go immediately to the hospital in Spokane for further tests."

I force my lips open, but my voice comes out very low. "Spokane?"

"They have the best facilities there ... You have to have more tests ... We just aren't equipped here to—"

"But I have a little baby!"

"You'll have to make arrangements for that."

My mouth is so dry, I can't speak. "This other doctor I went to, Doctor Thompson said it might be bursitis."

"I'm afraid Dr. Thompson was utterly mistaken."

"Why did he say it then?"

Dr. Lincoln shrugs. "I haven't the slightest idea, ignorance, probably."

"But shouldn't—I mean, if a doctor doesn't know, shouldn't he say that? Why should he pretend?"

"Mrs. Williams, let's focus on the present, shall we? Doctors aren't infallible . . . I'll call Dr. Wilde and tell him to expect you in a day or so."

"Okay, sure." I don't want to get up. It's like I know what lies ahead won't be good. This is bad, but it's the beginning. I want to just sit here. I don't want to go to Spokane. I almost wish I hadn't come to Dr. Lincoln, oh that's foolish, I know. But . . .

When I get out of the hospital, carrying Jill, there's Sam in his crazy old VW Jesus bus, all painted up with crazy designs on it. He opens the door and leans out. "Need a ride, pretty lady?"

I get in and close the door.

"Where are we going?" Sam says.

"Spokane . . . for tests. He thinks it's a tumor."

Sam looks so scared it scares me all over again. "Look, it's just a tumor, a mole, nothing!" He doesn't say anything. I can't get myself to even say the word "cancer". "I got to be there Monday."

Say something, Sam! Oh Christ, I feel so scared, it just hit me. I'm going to cry, don't let me, I'm crying. "Don't bail out, Sam. Not now."

He reaches over and hugs me tight, holds me. "Do you need the bus fare, girl, or do you need me?"

I start to laugh, even though I'm still crying. "How

can anyone be so stupid? How can I love anyone as stupid as you?"

Sam starts to laugh too. And Jill, seeing us both laughing, gives a big, toothless grin. What's the joke, Mommy and Daddy? What's so funny? You're too young to understand, baby. Just too young, that's all.

It's a pretty long drive to Spokane. A day and a half. Jill is real good, sleeps a lot. She seems to like looking out the window. I jiggle her up and down when she gets fussy. But I can't really think about her. I nurse her, but I keep thinking of what lies ahead and that's all I can think about. It's like being in some tiny room and on all the walls are the same thing so no matter how you turn, there it is. There's no door, you can't get out.

Sam said we should've left Jill with his parents. They live just outside Riverdale. I don't know. I guess we could've. But I want Jill with me. She's so important. Without her I don't feel like myself. Also, I know this sounds petty, but Sam's mother bugs me. I know she disapproves of our not being married, that to her, I seem like some loose woman who's living with her precious son. She knows I was married before, that Jill isn't illegitimate, but I know she thinks she is. Unless I brought David around to the house and introduced him

to her, she wouldn't really believe he ever existed. She
thinks I'm some kind of hippy because I wear my hair
loose and wear sandals—oh, all that crazy stuff. Maybe
all parents are like that.

I think it's worse because Sam is an only child. She
had him late in life. She'd been married fifteen years
and trying all the while I guess, and along he came. So
he's like Mama's little baby, even though he's twenty-
two. Sam is pretty good about it, I must say. He kind
of jokes with her, he sees her faults, he doesn't idealize
her. But I think he also doesn't see how much she disapproves of me. He doesn't want to, I guess. When I
told her, I was having natural childbirth, she kind of
stared at me like I'd said I was going to go out in the
fields and squat and have the baby on a pile of grass.
And the fact that Sam wanted to watch, she thought
was even crazier. In her day, the Daddy was kept far,
far away. He might faint or something. Anyway, I
think she also feels a man shouldn't see a woman "like
that", meaning real, sweating, in pain. It all ought to be
prettied up. Like the baby ought to be cleaned off and
powdered. And the Mommy too. Otherwise, "they" lose
respect, or some such crud.

Tests and more tests. X-rays, electrocardiograms, bi-opsy. From the time I enter the hospital, it's like my life, my real life—Jill, Sam—are put aside like some old bag. They move me back and forth, cart me around. None of it hurts exactly, it's the fear. I'm being a coward, I know. I shut it all out, as much as I can. David used to say that I had movies going in my head. I do, kind of. When I'm alone or on a bus or at the dentist, I just pull out one of my home movies and start watching it in my mind. It's great. I forget about everything. Sometimes, it's just made up things, some times real things, things I like remembering.

Like the day Sam and I met. I was so happy then. It was this gorgeous perfect day, hot, springtime. I was about four months pregnant, but I didn't show yet. No one knew. I was up in the mountains with some kids, friends. I didn't know most of them real well, just to hack around with. Everyone was spread out on the grass, eating, or playing music. I felt—I can't even describe it, but it was a mixture of being where it was so beautiful, the lovely day, being free—I'd left David about six weeks earlier—but mostly, being pregnant with Jill. I felt like Superwoman, like I could do anything; I was bursting with happiness. I liked the fact that no one knew I was pregnant yet but me, that I had this great terrific secret all to myself.

I never had morning sickness the way Darleen seemed to always have. I felt different, sleepy sometimes, but good, strong. I remember exactly where I was standing the minute I saw Sam. I was right outside the cabin handing this basket of bread around, and I just happened to look up and there was Weaver and this guy I'd never seen before pulling up on their bikes, guitars and stuff strapped on the back.

It was basically one of those dumb, crazy moments that you hear about, where you look at someone and you just "know". I mean, I guess love at first sight, except I don't believe in that. I don't believe in it but it happened. Oh, I know sometimes you feel that and you turn out to be dead wrong, the guy is some jerk. Sam isn't even so great looking. I mean, I love the way he looks, but I've met lots of handsomer guys who I didn't care about at all. I don't really like it if a guy is too handsome, not just because they're stuck up about it, but it's sort of lifeless, these guys with perfect teeth and hair. Sam had this wonderful, slow, kind smile and beautiful eyes, very warm, as though just seeing me had made his day. I smiled right back at him. Mom always used to say I shouldn't smile so much because my teeth are too big. When I smile, you see all of them practically, but I can't help it. I like to smile. I wanted him to know how I felt.

"Well, if it isn't old foul mouth himself," I called out. "Where you been, Weaver? It's been heaven without you."

"Mutual, baby," Weaver said. "You know Sam Hayden?"

"No, but I think I should."

Sam laughed, took his guitar and headed for the cabin. "Let me get a glass of water first," he said.

"I'll get it for you," I said.

"I'll get it."

"No, I'll get it." We ran in, kind of laughing, and I got there first, ahead of him, and gave him this big dipperful of water. I'm not always like that, if I meet a guy I like. Sometimes I'm much more shy and awkward. But it was being pregnant, it was everything. I just felt good, like there was no need to not show how I felt, not to be honest.

I think I kind of made Sam nervous. Now he says it made him feel great, but he looked a little like: wow, who *is* this girl! But he liked me, I could tell.

He sat down and began playing his guitar. It was the first time I heard him play. It was beautiful. I mean, I'd have loved him anyway, but I loved the way he played, the way he held the guitar. I just sat there, staring at him, looking at his face, his hands.

"You come on like this with everybody?" he said.

"Does it embarrass you? . . . It shouldn't."

"Why not?"

I liked that he was embarrassed. I liked teasing him and I knew he liked me. It was so good, that moment before anything had happened, when it was all ahead. Not that what's happened since hasn't been good, but that's the time I love to think back on. "Can I sit there?" I said finally. It was crazy, I just felt I wanted to be near him, to touch him. I guess I was coming on pretty strong, but at the time it didn't seem unnatural at all.

I sat next to him and he kept playing, but I could tell he was nervous. He kept looking at me and shaking his head. Later, Sam said he was feeling how come this had happened to him, what had he done. He said he couldn't quite believe it. Not that he hasn't had girls before, but, well—maybe it was more where he had to make a big play for them, which he says he hates to do. While we were sitting there, some people came in, and they'd look at us and then kind of edge out. I think we looked so happy, it embarrassed people.

Afterward, we took a long walk out in the mountains, just to get off by ourselves.

"What a place!" Sam said. "You been here long?"

"Here at the cabin? Don't I wish . . . I live in Riverdale, but I was born in Three Forks. You know Three Forks? It's right on the Columbia."

"I know," Sam said.

"I left home when I was sixteen," I said. "I was kind of a nervy little brat."

Sam smiled. We were lying on the grass. "I know, I *know!*" he said, and we were kissing and rolling around in the grass. I knew we'd make love, maybe right then, maybe that night, it didn't seem to matter when, it was gonna happen and be great. But I felt like I had to tell him first about the baby. So I pulled away a little. He said later that when I did that his heart sank, because he hadn't figured me for a tease and he was afraid I was going to suddenly come on different—about how we ought to wait till we knew each other better and all that.

"I have to tell you this one thing," I said. "I mean, I want you to know because I think—well, that people should be honest with each other about everything."

He kind of groaned and said, "If we have to be honest, I want you so goddamn much, right this minute!"

"I'm married—I mean I was, and I'm pregnant." I looked right at him. Some guys, that would turn them off. And if he was going to be one of them, I wanted to know right away, not after. Because after, it would hurt too much. I never could just sleep with a guy without falling in love, and I don't think that's bad, only—well, it makes me be more careful.

Sam sat up and looked away. I just sat watching him. It was so important, that moment, telling him. Because I knew I would find out something important about him too, and I just prayed it would be what I'd want.

"Who was it?" he asked.

"Why does everyone ask you *that* first? . . . That's such a dumb question! Ask me if I'm happy!"

"Was it Weaver?"

"Are you *kidding*? He's my cousin, and besides, I hate him. It's nobody here. I haven't seen him since I . . ." I was going to say ran away, but that sounded too young, like a kid, so I added, "since we were separated . . . I married him when I was sixteen. To get away from my mother, I guess."

"What about the baby?"

I lay back on the grass and looked up at the huge, blue sky. "Oh well, that's a whole other trip," I said, smiling.

"You're going to have it? You're going to keep it?"

I looked at him. "Sure I'm going to keep it . . . I want to be a mother more than anything else in the world. I always have."

I didn't mind that he asked me all those questions and that things right away got serious between us. I mean, we could have just gone off and made love and it would've been great and I could've told him then. But I liked that when we finally did make love—he knew, and it was like it was the three of us, making love together, the baby and me and Sam, all together. Being

pregnant just made it special. It really was like it was
our baby.

It probably seems crazy that I never told David I
was pregnant. In fact, even crazier, it was the day I
found out I was, that I decided to leave him. You'd
think it would be the opposite, that when you find out
you're pregnant, you get scared and need security and
figure—why not give a not so good marriage another
try. But I didn't feel that way. I felt stronger. Before I
was pregnant, I felt weak, like anything David said
made me feel so bad or so good. But after I knew, I
felt: the hell with you. Maybe I'd felt that deep down
all along and it took being pregnant to make it come
out. I didn't marry David just to get pregnant. I really
was in love with him or thought I was when we got
married. But even when things weren't so good with us,
I still wanted a baby. And I guess it sounds selfish, but
I didn't want to share it with him, I never told him,
even when I left that note for him and walked out. It
wasn't because I thought he'd holler and yell and try to
convince me I had to stay. He would've, but it wasn't
that. It was like as long as I didn't tell him, it was just
my baby, not his, not a part of our marriage. Sort of
the same way I *did* want to tell Sam. I feel really good
that Sam was the first person to know. It was something happening to the two of us, even if he hadn't
"done it". That didn't seem to matter. Jill is Sam's
baby, she really is.

Sam was so good when I gave birth. He was really
interested and read all the baby books with me. He
even read the part about how to deliver a baby at home
just in case it came fast which luckily Jill didn't. He
didn't mind that I got too fat, he said I was beautiful. I
knew I was too fat at the very end—I even had to take
my rings off because my fingers got swollen—but I

didn't mind it. I would usually, not being pregnant, but I guess at the time I felt like a real earth mother, and I'm not at all that type usually. Usually, I'm skinny and built more like a kid.

They let Sam stay with me while Jill was being born. He sat right near me and joked around and told stories and held my hand. This one bossy nurse kept trying to get him to leave. She said he'd make me nervous, and I said he wasn't. He kept teasing her. Every time she came in, he'd pretend to hide and say, "Don't make me go, nursie . . . Pretty please. I'll do anything you say." I love it when Sam clowns around. He can be like a child sometimes, but I get a kick out of it, like when he's happy and he'll jump and dance all around.

Now that Jill's six months old, I think back and wonder why I didn't worry more about things like: would she be born blind or deaf or with six toes. I just didn't. It never occurred to me I wouldn't have a perfect, beautiful baby girl. And I did! When they showed her to me, she was all slimy and wet and my heart kind of sank. I know newborns aren't pretty, but she looked so bad, I just kind of mumbled: take her away. Thank God they didn't.

Right after I gave birth, it was early morning and Sam went home to sleep. I should've been tired, I'd been up all night, but I was so high, I couldn't sleep. I've smoked grass and stuff, but I never had a high like the one I felt after Jill was born. It was weird, almost. I remember they brought me these magazines, just regular women's magazines which I wouldn't usually even bother to look at. But I would sit there and everything in the magazine would seem fantastic to me. It's hard to describe, but it was like the fact that there was such a thing as a magazine seemed amazing and the colors, the faces of the people in the ads. I'd sit there reading some recipe for chicken and it would leap out at me, I'd want to cry, it seemed so beautiful. It was tiring. I don't even know if I'd want to feel like that all the time. And I didn't. About two weeks later, I started coming down, slowly, not with a hard thump. I never felt depressed the way they say you can. But it was like, suddenly, magazines were just magazines again, the sky was just the sky. I could remember what it had been like, but I didn't feel it any more.

They say the maternity ward is the only happy place in the hospital, the only place where people are there because they want to be. That was sure true with me. I loved it. I wouldn't have liked to have my baby at home. The nurses were so nice, so friendly. When they brought Jill in the next day and the nurse handed her to me, I was scared I'd drop her. My hands were almost shaking, I was so excited.

"What do I do? How do I do it? Sam, look at her! She's gorgeous."

The nurse tried to settle Jill in just right. "Keep your arm under her head," she said.

Right away Jill made this little snap at my nipple and began to nurse. I felt so proud! "How does she know what to do? It's incredible! She was only just born!"

"It's hard work for her. She'll fall asleep in a minute. Don't worry if she only takes a little." She smiled at us. "I'll let you get to know each other."

Sam sat there, watching me nurse. We were both so happy, it was like you didn't want to talk because there wasn't anything to say. Just it, just being there, was the whole thing. Sam always starts to horse around when he feels that way—being that happy makes him embarrassed, the same way as that time we met. He said, "She looks like Adolf Hitler."

I laughed. "She looks like David."

There was sort of a silence and I wondered if I should've said that, even if it was true. I didn't want David to intrude on the three of us, even by mentioning his name, it just came out.

"Speaking of which," Sam said, "they gave me the birth certificate to fill out . . . . Where they said 'name of father', since I didn't know David's last name, I put Sam Hayden . . . Is that all right?"

I wanted to cry. I could feel tears in my eyes and I just reached up to hug him with the hand that wasn't holding Jill.

"All right," I whispered. "Oh wow. That's beautiful."

Some day I'll have Sam's baby. I want to so much. A little boy, a little girl, I don't care which.

I never pretend Sam and I are married. Some day maybe it'll happen, maybe not. I don't want Sam to ever feel he has to stay with me, out of duty or responsibility or anything. I felt that with David. That because I was so young and he'd taken me from the bosom of my family and all that, he felt I was like his responsibility. I can cope. I know I can. And if there isn't love between us, then let it be over. Maybe I say that now and later I won't, but I think I mean it.

Having been married, I know it isn't everything. It isn't nothing either. I'm not one of those people that feels marriage is dead and the thing to do is just go from one man to the next or be married four times. No, I like the idea of being with one man all my life, till I'm seventy or eighty or something being a grandma or even a great grandma. I don't mind the humdrum part of being with someone day after day. David thought it was that. He thought I was too young and I just wanted excitement and wasn't "mature enough". No, you were wrong, David. I like having the same guy come home to me every day and cooking for him and loving him. I mean, sure, I know after awhile you feel attracted to other men and you know if you would sleep with them, it would be good, but knowing you can't, that doesn't bother me. So I can't. If what you have is so good, like with Sam and me, it seems greedy to want any more. That's how I feel.

Love came softly
lowered its head,
You are my desire
come to my bed.

I followed an old road
and once 'round the bend
was met by an army,
come lend me your hand.

I fought many wars,
Spent time with a wound
have cried in the evening,
watched old flowers bloom.

'Tis time I shall leave thee,
Watched sunsets from other shores
and regret not giving
my love even more.

It's lunch time. The tests are all over. I'm sitting here looking at my lunch and I see Dr. Wilde coming toward the bed. I get this strange feeling. It's like when I was little and we were in the car and I thought the trees were moving. Daddy said—no, it's the car that's moving, the trees are really standing still. But I could see them coming at me, there was no way to stop them coming, I was sure *they* were the ones that were moving. I don't want Dr. Wilde to keep on walking over to my bed, to start talking, and I know he's going to, no matter what. I'm not God, I can't stop him.

He's Chinese, I guess, sort of longish hair, black eyes. Is he married? Does he have a baby? He's coming over, he's looking at my lunch.

"Want some tapioca?"

Without smiling, he says, "It looks delicious."

"Yeah." Say it, I'm watching him, I'm ready.

"You kids like it straight from the shoulder, don't you?"

I nod. Am I a kid? No, I feel older than that, but I must look like a kid to him.

He says, "You have something called osteogenic sarcoma. A tumor on the bone."

All those words are so scary, even though I'm not sure what they mean. I say, "But some tumors aren't so bad, right?" My voice is so low, he comes closer to hear me.

"This one's malignant. We need to stop it immediately ... I've rearranged my schedule and I'll operate tomorrow ... Osteogenic sarcoma is a kind of cancer that travels from bone to lung. If we do not stop it in the bone, we cannot stop it in the lung."

I lean back against the pillow. "Okay ... I see."

"Time is of the utmost importance," he says.

"Once it gets to the lung, I die, right?"

"Right."

There aren't any words, just a space, just a vacuum with fear floating around it, crashing around the sides of the room, like a blind person.

"How do you take a tumor out of a bone?"

He hesitates a second. "We take the bone off."

"My leg? You take my *leg* off?"

"It's the best way to try and stop the cancer."

"No! You can't!" The words just leap out of me from somewhere deep inside. Say something else. Please!

Very calmly he takes some papers out of his pocket and puts them on the bedside table. "I'm afraid you have no other options, Mrs. Hayden ... You'll have to sign these and give them to the nurse."

"What do they say?"

"That you give us permission for the operation."

"But I ... I have to talk to my—husband. I can't sign anything unless—where is he? Is he out there?"

"I didn't see him."

I hobble out to the hall. Sam isn't there. Oh God, Sam, Christ, where are you? Why aren't you here? What else is more important? I feel frantic. I need you, you bastard! Be here! Why did I say: my husband. How petty, how dumb. Why should I care if that doctor knows we're just living together? Maybe *he's* living with someone. Is my lover out there, this guy, this person I happen to love. Sam!

I can't find him, he's gone. Maybe for good. He's split, he's taken Jill. He doesn't want to face it. I don't blame him. Why should he? *I* have to, but he doesn't. He's going to just go, that's it.

God, that doctor, Doctor Wilde, was so cold! Just—cut off your leg! No other option. I mean, there's got to be. In this day and age, with all those medicines they have! He didn't seem to give a damn. Oh why should he, I guess? Who am I to him? I don't even know if he's right. What if they cut off my leg and it turns out they could've done something else?

Waiting for Sam. He's got to come. He will, won't he? Deep down I don't think he's split. I just said that, thought it. He'll come back. I'm in a ward with some other patients—one has polio, another one had his appendix out, another has a broken hip. God, there are so many ways to be sick, to be deformed, to die. So many ways. I don't want to think about it, I don't want to even be here.

I get dressed. I have to keep off my leg, it hurts. I feel weak, kind of. Maybe all the blood they took for the tests. And I've been losing weight. I know I'm thinner, I haven't weighed myself, but I can tell. My pants are loose around the waist. I feel frantic, I've *got* to get out of here! I hate this place!

All of a sudden Sam comes in, carrying Jill.

"Finally!" I say. I hear my voice, too shrill. I'm shaking, I'm so angry, upset.

"What's up?"

"Why weren't you *here*? I needed you!"

He holds me, tries to calm me down, but it doesn't work. I feel like I'm going to explode if I don't get out of here, right this second!

"Hey, hang on, lady! Slow down ... what's going on?"

"They want to amputate my leg."

He stiffens. "No."

"Tomorrow."

"Come on—"

"Right, big joke ... Sam, let's get out of here, okay? Please, right this second, right now. I've gotta think, I've got to get up to the mountains."

"What do they want to amputate your leg for?"

"Because it's full of *cancer*," I yell.

Oh, it's not Sam's fault. Why am I yelling at him? It's no one's fault, but least of all is it Sam's. But I want—someone to share the pain, to help me take it.

That's what Mom always said. Whenever things go wrong: take it easy, but take it ... take it.

A summer's pasture
at my gate
beckons me astray—
to places found
in lovers' dreams
and easy winter days

Sky of liquid
dyed blue scenes
follow close upon my mind
long dark trains
of empty clouds
and simple musical strains.
lots of fruit and willow trees
follow from behind.
dreams.
Dreams.

The mountains are so beautiful. It's hot, there are flowers all around. The whole hospital thing didn't happen. This is what's real. How could this be real and that too? It can't be.

We go out with Jill during the day and she crawls around with no clothes on. There's the smell of the flowers, the sound of bees and grasshoppers.

I wonder if there's a God. "Well honey," I remember Mom saying when our old dog, Grey, got hit by a truck: "He had to die sometime and God will be so glad to have such a big nice doggie in heaven."

I was six at the time and I'd seen it happen, seen these people in an old pink Rambler purposely swerve over to hit my dog.

"Does everybody go to heaven, Mommy?"

"Yes, honey, and someday you will too. Just always remember that God will be waiting for you, and there is nothing to be afraid of . . ."

Much as I wanted to believe her, I was scared as hell. I didn't want to go up there and see old Grey, even though I missed him.

How am I supposed to react? What do I do? Should I cry? Just keep going, I guess. If thousands of Jews can burn in ovens and young men can go to war, somewhere in this heart of mine there'll be the courage to go on. There has to be.

I lie here, and the sun is so hot and my baby is so beautiful, and Sam . . . Maybe that time in the hospital was a dream, like that one I had that night. It was last night and now I've woken up.

Sam puts a daisy chain on my head.

"Where did you learn to make those?"

"Girl scout camp."

I laugh and lean back. "The sun feels good."

"Dr. Wilde said a lot of heavy stuff there."

"He's a freak."

"You want to go to another doctor?"

"I don't want to talk about it."

"Every doctor we've seen's said something different ... Maybe we should go to the Niles Cancer Clinic."

"In Vancouver?"

"So, a couple of hundred miles, that's not so much."

"I want to stay right here, just like this, for the rest of my life. I'm happy ... Oh, shut up, okay?"

He looks away and pulls some sandwiches out of the basket. "Want a peanut butter and jelly?"

"I want some peace and quiet."

He takes out his camera and starts taking photos. Sam takes great photos. I never could. We have some wonderful ones of Jill. We found this great way to get her to laugh for a photo. You just hiccup. She thinks that's a riot. She laughs like a baby hippo, with her whole mouth open.

"Baby, you're getting kind of fat," Sam says.

"What'd you mean? She only has three chins."

"I think there's a fourth one sneaking in there."

He keeps snapping away. Jill crawls over on my stomach. "She is kind of heavy, now that you mention it ..."

"Hold her ... There, that's it, that's terrific."

She begins picking at my daisy chain. "All your hard work, honey."

He smiles. "I'll make another one."

"Should we let her eat the petals? Is it good for her?"

"Sure, it's good. It's great. Nothing like daisy petals to make a baby grow up nice and strong."

Am I not going to see my baby grow up? I never thought of that before this second. No, why would God do that. He doesn't need me, why should he bother? I remember this poem we learned in school by Edgar Allen Poe about this girl, Annabel Lee. She died and he said the gods were jealous of them. Are you jealous of us, God? Don't be. We fight, we have problems, we don't have much money, Sam doesn't even have a job. You don't have to be jealous of us.

Sam is looking at me. "Sweetheart."

"Are we too happy? Is that why?"

"Uh uh." He lies down next to me and holds my hand. The three of us lying in the sun. It's real, we have it now, forget about the rest.

I believe there is a God, but I don't know why I do. Just because it's been harped at me all my life? Maybe. Also because I've seen things happen that I can't explain. I believe that Jesus might have really lived and those things they say he did might've really happened. But I don't know about heaven. I think Jesus meant we had to love each other on earth because earth is our heaven. Earth is imperfect, but it has to be. I don't think we'd want some perfect place, some heaven with streets paved in gold and water sparkling out of streams. It has to be here, if it's anywhere.

I think I'm too human to even enjoy a place like heaven is supposed to be. I wouldn't enjoy "perfection." I like making mistakes, learning from them. I like knowing what's happening. I learned from being married to David, even if it didn't work out.

I know we'll have to go back to some hospital, maybe the one in Vancouver. I can't wish it away. But I want these days to sink in, as deep as they can. When we're making love, I want to feel every second, more than I did before. I want to show Sam I love him. Even if he wants to split after this, if things get worse, okay. Let him. I'll understand. I don't want him to feel my love as a burden, dragging him down. I just want him to know someone loved him this much. I want him to have that. Because he deserves it, he's so good, he's so kind.

I wish this weekend could be forever. Just walking around, going barefoot, wearing buttercups in my hair. Getting up at dawn and watching the sun rise. Letting Jill root around in the grass. Everything is new to her now. She'll sit there holding a flower and just staring at it. Babies must be stoned all the time. She just sits and looks and turns it over. No sense of—gee, I'm wasting time, I ought to be doing something else. I learn so much from her. I think babies are wise.

One night we take a blanket outside and lie looking up at the sky, the stars. There're shooting stars now, lots of them. If you lie there like that, the sky is so big, you feel so little.

"Listen, Sam—"

"Umm."

"If . . . well, if you want to split, do it now, okay? I don't mind, I really won't . . . I can get to Vancouver."

"You really think a lot of me, huh?"

"No, I don't mean it that way . . . I just want you to feel free."

"I do."

"No, like, sense of responsibility . . . like you used to say when your uncle was dying and it took so long and your aunt had to—"

"Honey, this is different."

"It might not be." I wish I could say this right, my words come out all wrong. "Well, just promise, if you ever want to go, you will, right?"

"Sure." He's holding me and the blue-black sky seems the whole world. If I could die now. No, I don't want to. Even if I could, I still . . .

"I hope I can still have more babies ... Do you think I can?"

"I just don't know, honey."

"I could get pregnant right away ... No, Jill's too little, it wouldn't be fair to her, I guess ... I want to be with her more ... What do you think the perfect age gap would be? Maybe two years."

"That sounds good."

"I don't care about getting married, that doesn't matter ... You'd be great with a little boy."

"Yeah, I'd like that."

I can imagine Sam with a son so well. He'd be gentle. He wouldn't make him feel he had to act rough and tough to be a man. He'd teach him just the right way to be. He'd show him things. He'll do that with Jill too, of course, but I think he'd be especially good with a boy. He'd have curly hair, like Sam. He said he was a redhead when he was little. I love real carroty-red hair.

Sunday's our last day. Monday morning we're heading for Vancouver. It's a good day, we're outdoors all the time. Jill's getting a sunburn, but not too red. She doesn't seem to have delicate skin, even though her hair is light. I put some baby oil on her just to be careful.

As we're coming home for supper, I see someone sitting on the bench in front. It's David. I can tell right the second I see him, even though he's turned away. How did he get here? How did he—No, damn it, I don't want him here!

Sam, in his usual way, gives a big smile, "Peace . . . Welcome . . . What's your name?"

He could be someone come to kill us, Sam . . . Why does he always expect people to be nice? "It's David," I say under my breath.

"No, can't be," he says, loud enough for David to hear. "He doesn't have fourteen heads and green scaly skin."

That's so much like Sam, to say something like that loud enough for David to hear. Maybe to Sam I have made David out worse than he was, I'm not sure. Just to justify my leaving. I don't think leaving itself was so bad, but maybe it was childish just going off, leaving a note. Only I had tried to explain before that, I'd tried a million times and David just wouldn't listen. He just never took it seriously. If he had, if he'd even bothered to argue with me or discuss it, maybe we'd still be together. In that way I'm almost glad he didn't because then I'd never have met Sam.

David just sits there, watching us come closer. I feel like some big hand in my stomach is tightening up. Go away, David! Vanish into a cloud of smoke. I have a magic power to just look at someone and transport them millions of miles away. There! Oops, he's still there.

"What'd you come here for?" I say, trying not to sound angry, trying to be calm.

"To see my child," he says, fixing me with a stare. Why does he do that to me? He makes me shrivel up inside with that look, I hate it.

"She's not yours ... She's mine," I say, knowing I sound childish.

"Your mother told me about her," he says. "It never occurred to her that I didn't know."

Damn her! Why did she have to tell him? She's never even come to see Jill, that's how much she cares about her. What business is it of hers to tell him? It's so crazy. I always felt Mom thought David was too good for me. Can you imagine? I don't think I'd think any man ever was good enough for Jill, but Mom, she practically tried to convince David not to marry me! Like, he didn't know what he was getting into, he should finish his studies first. Not a word about me.

Oh, they got along swell. I bet they had a great time talking about me after I left him. I can just picture it, what a mess I am and was, always was, all the crap both of them have had to put up with because of me. Damn them both!

"I signed the divorce papers," David said.

"You've only had them like a year."

"But I signed them before I knew about the child."

"Her name's Jill," Sam says.

"He doesn't need to know her name," I say, angry at both of them, but more at Sam.

"Look, she has a name, she's not 'the child' . . . Why shouldn't he know it?" To David Sam says, smiling, "She's Jill Patricia Hayden . . . Jill for her paternal grandmother, Patricia for Kate's younger sister and Hayden for me." He cocks his head to one side. "She looks like you. Kate said she did when she was born."

"I'd like to spend some time with her," David says.

"Come on in, then . . . Have some supper with us."

"I'd like that."

Oh, this is wonderful. Sam, what's wrong with you? Can't you see what I'm feeling? How can you be so nice to everybody?

We go inside. I don't say anything. I just stand there, biting my lips, feeling betrayed and alone. Sam genially hands Jill to David. She's so good with strangers she just sits there, smiling. Scream, yell, baby! Oh, everyone is betraying me! No, she's just a baby. He could be the man in the moon to her.

I go into the bedroom and Sam goes after me. "Go away," I say.

"Baby, come on . . . Does it hurt to act civilized?"

"It hurts *me*."

"No, it'll be good."

"It *hurts,* Sam!"

He holds me. He's so good, Sam. He can't know what it's like, he's never been married before and I think that is different than just having lived with someone—and I'm the only person he's ever even lived with. You do commit yourself with marrying someone, and it can get ugly in that special way of feeling trapped. Maybe that could happen somewhat the same with living with someone, but I think it would still be a little different.

Supper. I don't talk. What should I say? I just sit there, looking at the two of them and listening to them. It's interesting, if I wasn't so tight inside, to see Sam and David together. David is better looking—I'm sure most women would think that. Even here, even just spreading mustard on his bread he has that thoughtful, serious, I know just what I'm doing air. Sam seems kind of funny, clowning around. There's a kind of sweetness in Sam—that might seem a funny word to use for a man, but I feel he wants so much for David and me to make up, like he was our mother or something. Instead of being jealous the way some guys might—this is my woman. No, he'd never do that. That's not his way.

"It ought to be possible, theoretically at least, for two people to love each other," Sam says, "then stop, but still talk. They're still people, right? Why not be honest—just forget all the rest. It's over. Just deal with what's up front, the practical stuff."

"Sure," I say.

David says nothing, just goes on munching on his sandwich.

Sam raises his hand and gestures like an actor. "Never let it be said that man, in the quest of peace and love and understanding, be it ever so humble, quests in vain."

David looks at me with a wry expression. "What's he on?"

"Nothing." I can't help smiling. "He just gets this way."

"Spooky," David says.

"I like it," I say, looking right at him.

Silence again. This is really a great dinner.

"Your car was packed," Sam says. "Where you headed?"

"Pullman, the university."

Sam looks at David admiringly. "Can you cut that? What're you studying?"

"Geology," David says.

Sam, you're worth ten thousand million Davids no matter how many dumb degrees he has. Don't you know that, you idiot?

David is looking at me. "I talked to a lawyer," he said. "Not telling me you were pregnant when you filed for divorce is what they call an omission of a material fact . . . which means I don't have to agree to the divorce. And I can get custody of the child."

I just plain don't believe this. No one would be that cruel. I can't even believe he's right. What kind of law is that? To give a baby to her father who never gave a shit about children, who didn't even *want* them. David always said the world was too rotten, he didn't want to tie us down. I always thought maybe if I got pregnant, he'd go along with it, accept it, but he never wanted it, never. "You can't have her," I say.

"Why do you want her, anyway?" Sam says. "Are you big on babies?" He says it in his innocent way, kind of wondering, the way he asked about David's studying. It's a little of an act, Sam's not really innocent. He's putting David on a little.

"I'm not saying I want her," David says. "I'm saying I can have her."

Sam looks at me. "I see what you mean about him."

David won't pay any attention to Sam, like he wasn't there. Maybe he knows I'm more vulnerable. If Sam wasn't here—no. I don't even want to think of that, I'd be screaming, I'd be hysterical. I'm like that inside now, but just having Sam here makes me able to keep it down. "Frankly, I don't know why *you* want a baby," David says to me. "How come you didn't have an abortion?" To Sam he says, "All I heard for a year and a half was—lemme out! I'm trapped, this is an awful mistake, I'm tied down, I hate making your bed, ironing your shirts, I hate responsibility, I'm not ready—"

"Shut up!"

I hate David when he gets going like that. He can massacre me with words, relentless, going at me, distorting everything. "Here you are, taking care of a house, a man and a child . . . What happened? What was the great miracle?"

"I wear t-shirts," Sam says.

"I grew up," I say. I could say: it's different when you love someone, but aside from being cruel that isn't even true, I mean, it's not the real difference. It's that Sam doesn't care about those things, he doesn't make me feel like I'm a person he bought to do chores around the house and he'll fire me if I don't act right. Partly, he just doesn't care about all that, the way David did, does, but also he feels it's my thing. If I want to—fine. And once you don't feel you have to, it's not a burden. I really like housework, crazily enough. I mean, not to spend all day at it, but I like the house to be clean and nice, so long as I don't feel someone is making me or will be angry if one morning I want to lie in bed and write a poem instead of defrosting the refrigerator.

"I'm really impressed," David is saying. "No, it's a real miracle . . . To grow up in one year from a little, whiny kid to—"

"Why did you marry me if I was a little, whiny kid?"

"You weren't like that when I married you!"

"Well, maybe—"

"Hey, kids, cool it," Sam says.

We both glare at him.

"I mean, I don't like to be insulting," Sam says, "but speaking of little kids, you two are not exactly—"

"Look, maybe Kate is a great mother right now," David says. "It's possible . . . But what happens when the next great transformation occurs? When some other life style strikes her fancy? Then what?"

"That's unfair," Sam says.

"Is it fair to raise a child when you're stoned on grass or whatever half the—"

I get up. "I don't believe this . . . That's the stupidest thing I've ever heard! It's not even true!" As though I was some hippy out of a book. He sounds like my mother. Either you're straight and narrow or you're a wild, drooling, grass-smoking maniac who's a danger to little babies. How did I marry someone like this?

"I'll give you the divorce, if you'll give me Jill," David says. "I'll raise her right. My mother will. You know her, Kate. You like her. She'll raise her right, won't she? . . . And you'll have what you've always wanted. Freedom. A new start. No responsibilities."

I start to cry. He can't do that, he just can't. He can't take my baby. I won't let him.

Sam says, "Listen, Jill needs Kate, Kate needs Jill. I need them both . . . Does that make sense to you?"

"Why don't we go outside and talk it over?" David says.

"You're kidding, come on ... why can't we talk here? This involves Kate."

"I'd rather do it my way," David says.

Sam makes a comic face and straggles out after David.

They're going to kill each other. Oh, how dumb, how awful. Please God, I know I said I don't believe in everything about you like heaven and all that, but if you exist, don't let him take Jill. Okay? I won't ask for any other thing, I promise. Just that.

I walk in and look at her. She's sleeping on her back. Babies sleep in such a vulnerable way, on their backs like that with their arms and legs spread out, like a puppy wanting you to rub his stomach. She's in a little, pink stretch suit which is getting tight around her neck because of her chins. I guess she needs an extra large already. She never has a blanket—she just kicks it off, and the stretch suit is wool, it's warm enough. My puss, he never even said anything about you, he never said how pretty, how good. He just held you like a sack of potatoes.

Sure, I like David's mother. I do, really. I like her more than David actually. Maybe because I think she thinks he's kind of a square too, kind of rigid. And he thinks she's kind of kooky because she goes on marches against the war and says she was a feminist before her time. She is great, but she's—well, she's sixty and that's too old! And even if she were forty, that's not the point. I want my baby. Maybe he's right. Maybe when I was with him I was all those things, but I am different now. Why can't he see that? Because he doesn't want to think it was him who was making me that way?

He doesn't want Jill! He doesn't even want her! He wants to hurt me, that's all. I don't want to hurt you, David. I just want you to go away and never come back. I'm not even asking you for alimony or child support. You're the one who can be free and go live in some nice apartment and travel like you said you wanted and maybe later marry some lady geologist who would give parties the way you wanted. What would *you* do with a baby?

I can hear David's car starting up outside. Well, at least one of them is alive. No, that was silly. Sam doesn't even like fighting. He's said that when he was little, they all made fun of him because he never liked to fight. Didn't believe in it, he wasn't scared.

He comes back in the house.

"Who killed who?"

"We killed each other."

I start giggling. I feel so happy to have it over, to have David gone. "Come on, tell me, what happened?"

"He understood."

"Really?" Suddenly I look at him. He has a funny expression on his face. "Did you tell him about my— did you tell him I was sick?"

Sam nods.

"Oh Sam, why? Why does he have to know that?"

"I don't know . . . I think it's important."

"You mean, any other time it would be okay for him to take Jill, but not now that I'm sick?"

"No, honey, come on . . . We wanted her, we have her . . . That's the important thing, right?"

"Yeah, I guess." I sigh. "He's sweet, isn't he?"

"Adorable . . . You have wonderful taste in men."

"Wow." I pick up a piece of bread and butter. Suddenly, I feel hungry, I didn't eat anything at dinner.

"Is that what he was usually like?"

I take a sip of wine. "Not every second . . . But I'm glad you saw it. I mean, otherwise you might've thought that I was making it up—"

"No, I wouldn't have."

Goodbye, David. Good try.

The Niles Clinic is the best. We decide to go there and see. It's a long drive again to Vancouver. Sam drives, I sit next to him, holding Jill. She looks out the window, smiles, makes these strange crooning sounds to herself, like a bird. I wonder what she sees. She doesn't know where we're going, that we're in a car, that those are trees, what a mountain is. But it must mean something to her, she keeps talking to herself in her bird language, gesturing her fat, little hands like she was conducting a symphony.

We sing some of the time, we talk. But we don't talk about where we're going or why we're going there. Deep down I know it's not going to be different, it'll be the same tests, the same kind of doctors' faces, cold, straight, not caring. But I feel they have to have some answer besides cutting off my leg. Here there's always all this stuff in the paper about cancer and trying to cure it. They must have gotten further than just saying

cut off your leg. If it was my breast—well, I wouldn't
mind so much. Oh, I would mind it, but—it's not being
able to get around, being a cripple. Nobody would see
with a breast, except Sam and he—well, I don't know
how he'd feel. But with a leg, everyone could see. Jill
would see me that way. Don't let me be a coward. I
don't want to be. I just want to grow up and take care
of Jill and Sam. That's all. Is it such a huge amount to
ask for?

The Niles Clinic is very big. For several days I go
through all the tests again. They give me something
called a bone scan. They inject a radioactive drug in the
vein of my arm. Then a day or so later, they put me
under a machine that detects the hot spots or the places
where the radioactive material has gone to, which indi-
cates the more active parts of the tumor. I lie there for
an hour, I can't tell how long, as still as I can, and
this arm of the machine moves back and forth above
me, detecting the hot spots and recording them on
film.

They take a scintiscan of my liver. It's like having an
ordinary black and white Polaroid Color Pack II
mounted on a $50,000 computer that can take pictures
of anything—the heart, the brain. There, they show it
to me—a little black and white snapshot of my liver.
Incredible!

I try to run my home movies in my mind, but they
keep flickering out and the faces of the doctors come
in. I have to tell my story so many times, when I first
noticed the bump, what the other doctors said, when
the first x-rays were taken. Over and over.

They put a crib and a folding bed into my room so
that Sam and Jill can stay with me which is good except that sometimes having Sam around gets on my
nerves. I don't feel like joking or even talking. Then,

when I do, when I want him, he's not around. Am I going through this every time with him? Here one minute, gone the next? Sam, come on!

Dr. Gillman, the head doctor, sees me in the corridor. "You shouldn't be up, Kate," she says. "You need to keep your weight off that leg."

It's funny to me, a woman in charge of a whole cancer section. I mean, I know women are doctors, but I never went to one or even heard of anybody going to one. Can she be good? How awful, that's so prejudiced, but I wonder if a woman can be as good a doctor, know as much ... But I like her. She reminds me of my grandmother, Dad's mother, who stayed with us for about a year before she died. That sounds funny since Dr. Gillman is only in her thirties or something and my grandmother was in her seventies. It's something about her eyes, her voice, very quiet and sure. I used to come into my grandmother's room after school. She'd be sitting there, working on her patchwork quilts. She'd let me help her, I'd trim the patches out and she'd hem them. I think it got on Mom's nerves, having her live with us. She said we didn't have room enough and Grandma was always in her way. But Dad loved her and didn't want to put her in some home where they were all so sick, some with strokes and things like that. It seemed cruel. Toward the end, she got sort of senile. She used to go around wearing maybe six petticoats at once because she was afraid someone might steal her things, and she was always losing things and wandering off and getting lost. I guess she was a bother for Mom, but I always loved her.

"Are you a good doctor?" I say suddenly.

Dr. Gillman smiled. "Very good ... Why?"

"I never had a woman doctor."

"Don't you think women can be good doctors?"

"I guess I . . . I don't know . . . Did they put you in charge of this part because we're all hopeless cases?"

"Because this is the children's wing." She smiles at me. "Children who don't stay in bed when they're told to stay in bed."

"My bottom gets sore," I say defensively.

"I'll have them bring you a crutch."

"Great."

What I like about Dr. Gillman, compared to that doctor in Spokane, is she treats me like a person. He treated me like a thing, like a "case." I mean, I know all patients are cases to doctors, they can't get personally involved every time, but it makes such a difference when they look at you like they care, like you're important to them, even a little bit.

She comes back after lunch and sits near my bed. "We better talk about your treatment," she says.

I'm so scared again. For awhile it went away, now it comes back suddenly, like someone just threw a hood over my head. "Don't cut off my leg," I say. My mouth is dry. I lick my lips, watching her.

"The scanner showed it may not have spread to any other parts of your body which is amazing considering how long you waited."

"I didn't wait, though! I went, only they said—"

"No, I know . . . You did wait a little, however."

"I was pregnant, though, and—"

"I understand, Kate . . . And those doctors who told you you had bursitis, that's very unfortunate. That kind of mis-diagnosis is still possible. I regret it very much . . . But that's all over. And for now, amputation is your best option."

"Will it get rid of the cancer?"

She hesitates. "It might."

"But if it hasn't spread—"

"It's a chance, Kate . . . I won't lie to you. That's all it is, a chance."

"Why can't they cure it, some other way, for good?"

"Some day they will."

"But it won't do *me* any good, right?"

"These things take a long time, finding out what cancer is will take a long time, how to cure it is something else again."

"So I'll be one-legged and dying. Terrific."

"Your only other option is chemotherapy and radiation. Radiation to kill the cancer in the bone. Drugs to stop it spreading to other parts of your body . . . The possible side effects of radiation you know about. From the drugs you may have loss of hair, diarrhea, nausea."

"Will I be able to have more children?"

"No, you won't, Kate, I'm sorry."

"Never?"

"No."

I look away. Don't let me cry, please! Oh Christ, let me be strong, I've got to be! I feel Dr. Gillman's kind, worried eyes on me. I can't speak.

"Kate?"

"Have you noticed that Sam is never here when I need him?" I say suddenly, the words bursting out. "That's true. Never. Mr. Vanishing Act . . . You know where he is? Auditioning. He goes off to some damn audition right when I need him. What's more important, country western music or my life? Country western music, hands down."

"He needs a job, Kate," Dr. Gillman says kindly. "He wants to take care of you. He can't do that without a job."

"But I need him *here*!"

I go out to the phone and try to call the place where Sam's auditioning. I hate phone booths, operators, switchboards. It's so humiliating to keep calling and get no answer. "No, I'm sorry, we don't know where he can be reached . . ." Fuck them! I can't have more children, Sam! I'll never have your baby! Don't you care? Why aren't you here? I lean back and close my eyes.

Suddenly, I see Sam, walking past the phone booth with Jill in the back pack. He doesn't see me. I just sit there and a minute later he comes back. I look up at him.

"You look like you could use some music, lady," he says.

I just glare at him.

"Come back to bed . . . You're not supposed to be up."

"How do you know?" I follow him. I feel so full of bitter, ugly, sad feelings. My leg is hurting. It does feel better to get in bed.

Sam takes out his guitar and begins picking at it. He's put Jill in her crib in the corner of the room.

"I can't make any sensible decision without you and you're never here," I say.

"This morning you said I was getting on your nerves."

"Well, I didn't need you while I was having the tests . . . Any idiot could figure *that* out!"

He keeps strumming on the guitar.

"Stop hiding behind that stupid guitar!"

He's hurt. His face goes blank and he puts the guitar down. "Look, Kate, how much more money do you think I want to borrow from my parents?" he says, angry. "I've got to get a job, I've—"

"Oh, cut it out. You could get a job any day in the week if you wanted. Washing dishes. Mopping floors. Driving a truck. But you don't. You just want to get away. From me, from this whole scene ... 'Cause you're too weak to—"

"Get away? Right, great, I've just been staying here, sleeping at the foot of your bed ever since you checked in for fun! I sort of dig hospitals, right?"

"You don't have any place else to sleep, for free."

"Quit it!"

Why am I doing this? Oh, I don't need the pain of wrecking what there is between Sam and me. Am I angry just because he isn't sick, because he has so many options, getting a job, not getting one, because he has two strong legs and no one wants to cut either of them off, no one is piping him full of radioactivity.

Jill is fussing and I go to get her. I can feel Sam watching me. I hurt him, I know it. He's angry. Oh, I wish we could just lie down together and love each other like we used to. I can imagine us together, as I'm picking up Jill, it's as though I was with Sam and we were out in some meadow and the sun was shining.

Holding Jill makes me feel good, better anyway. She's so fat and soft and she doesn't hate me or look at me with angry eyes. I snuggle her up to my breast, cradling her. I can't look at Sam, I just can't.

Suddenly, Dr. Gillman comes in. "Don't let her nurse," she says to Sam.

Talk to *me*! It's *my* baby! "But she—"

"You have radioactive iodine in you from the tests. It can be passed in your milk ... Take her off your breasts."

I pull Jill away and she begins to cry. I feel like I'm dying. Please don't take my baby away! How horrible, that my body is filled with poison, that my milk is contaminated. "I wasn't going to wean her till she was ... I—"

"I'll get a bottle," Dr. Gillman says.

Jill and I are both crying. She's hungry and frustrated, I feel like I want to curl up and pull the blankets over my head. Oh, it's not fair! Sam stands near the bed, stroking Jill's head. "Should I take her?" he says softly. "Should I hold her?"

"Go away."

"I thought I was never around when you needed me?"

"Get out."

Dr. Gillman comes in with a bottle. She props me up with some pillows. "Sit up, more, Kate . . . Now it's perfectly easy. You just hold her as you would if you were nursing, and give her the bottle . . . And stop crying."

I can't stop, the tears keep rolling down my cheeks. Jill doesn't want the bottle. She turns away. Even she's angry at me!

"She won't take it."

"Let me," Sam says.

"No!"

I hold Jill against me. Sam looks at me, incredulous. I see Dr. Gillman glance at him. "You know, it might be a good idea to let Sam feed her, Kate . . . With you she's used to the breast. Babies often take bottles from their fathers and—"

"He's *not* her father," I say bitterly. "He's not my husband, either."

Dr. Gillman takes Jill and gives her to Sam. He sits down with the bottle. "Is this the way?" he says.

"Hold her head up a little more," she says. "There, now look . . . She's used to it already!"

"But it's not the same as nursing," I say.

"Not exactly . . . But the baby feels you love her just

as much. Babies aren't dumb. They can tell if they're loved."

I feel jealous, watching Sam feed Jill. She does look perfectly at home in his arms, like he was her mother.

"I thought I understood that Jill's last name was the same as yours?" Dr. Gillman says to Sam.

"It is . . . Kate was married before, but she left her husband before Jill was born."

"She obviously feels you're her father," Dr. Gillman says, smiling warmly.

He smiled back at her. "Yeah, well, I—"

"I actually think bottle feeding has a lot of advantages," she says. "Why should the mother have all the fun? I think it's nice for the baby to get to know that lots of people care about her and love her."

"So, if anything happens to the mother, she won't—" I start to say, but Dr. Gillman says, "Just so she feels all her happiness isn't just one person."

I guess I *want* her to feel all her happiness is me, that's selfish, I know. And Sam does look so sweet, feeding her, so awkward, but sort of pleased with himself. He glances at me just one second, as though to get my approval, and then away. But I still feel too tight inside, I can't let go.

"Have you two discussed your treatment yet?" Dr. Gillman says.

Sam looks at me. "*I'd* like to," he says.

"Well, the generally accepted way to treat osteogenic sarcoma is by amputation. You remove the cancerous part. If it hasn't spread, it's the best solution."

"He's not interested."

Sam makes a disgusted face and looks away.

"The other possibility," Dr. Gillman says, "is radiation and chemotherapy."

"Which will cause my hair to fall out, my leg to break, diarrhea, and nausea," I say, bitter.

"Possibly," says Dr. Gillman, "but I don't know that you can compare losing your hair with losing your leg."

"It's a lousy trip either way," I say, looking at both of them. "Why don't we skip the whole bit?"

They are both staring at me like I'm crazy. I feel crazy, no, not crazy, just full of ugliness, of hate at the unfairness of it. And their kindness makes it worse, somehow. I guess I want to blame someone and they're the only ones patient enough to sit here and listen to me ranting.

"That's suicide," Sam says, his eyes cold and angry again.

Why can't he understand? Is it so clearcut? Would he just have his leg cut off in one second like that without caring? "But all these horrible things she's going to do to me," I say, my voice shaking a little, "And no guarantees!"

"No guarantees," Dr. Gillman says, "but a little more time." She looks over at Jill who is sucking away on the bottle—she really seems to like it. "Time for this one . . . I thought that's what you wanted—to be a mother."

I curl up in bed, away from both of them, all of them, even Jill. I wish I could explain how I felt. I know they both think I'm acting childish, unrealistic, immature. Okay, maybe I'm too young, so why am I sick, why am I dying? I'm too young for that, so why did it happen? If they can't understand, no one will and I can't bear that somehow. I can't bear that cold look in Sam's eyes. If only someone could say why this was happening. There is no why, I guess. Do I want there to be? Would that make it better? To have some-one say: this is because you were born on the thirteenth, this is because you ran away from home, because you made your first husband miserable, because your mother thinks you're a whore . . . That's childish, to want life to be a matter of "punishment" for one's sins, but to have it just happen, at random, and for no reason, that's almost worse. Oh, I don't know what I want anymore. Except to be left alone, to try and figure it out. I turn around and look at them. "It's just," I try and keep my voice steady. "I don't want to be a temporary mother, for a year or two. I want to be a mother until I'm a grandmother . . . I can't learn to walk on one leg while Jill's learning to walk on two, I won't . . . It's not fair to Jill."

After my big announcement, Jill gives a decisive burp. So much for you and your dramatic words, Mom. Sam pats her back. She looks very pleased with herself.

"What does all that mean, in practical terms?" Dr. Gillman says.

Sam smiles, but he doesn't look angry anymore, his voice is gentle. "It means she wants to wake up tomorrow with no cancer."

I try to joke, too. "And three legs, please. Certainly not any less than two."

Dr. Gillman nods, as though she were satisfied. "Fine. Then we'll start radiation treatment in the morning."

I feel so relieved she understood that I want to cry. I look at Sam. Jill is almost asleep, nodding in his arms. "Can I hold her?"

"Sure." He gives her to me and she settles against me, warm, milky. "She drank the whole thing," he says proudly.

"She's going to be a fat girl, aren't you?" I say, pressing one finger lightly on her cheek. "All that milk . . ."

"Would you two call a truce if I sent in two din-ners?" Dr. Gillman says, from the door.

"Sure," Sam says.

"No." I say.

They both look at me, surprised.

I smile teasingly. "I'm not hungry," I say.

Dr. Gillman shakes her head. "You're impossible," she says, but in a nice way. I really like her. Maybe all doctors should be women.

After she leaves, Sam comes over and sits right next to me on the bed. I suddenly feel physically aware of him, wanting him. I imagine us together in this bed. He doesn't touch me, just sits very close, but it's as though we were touching. "Why is it tangled up, all of a sud-den?" he says.

"I don't know."

He takes my hand and kisses it. There are marks there, from the shots. "I love you . . . Did you forget that?"

"No. It's just that . . . I don't know."

"Say it."

"I'm scared."

"I know . . . I am too. Everybody is, baby, inside, always."

"Maybe she's wrong . . . Maybe there's another doc-tor somewhere else who'll have another answer."

He frowns, hesitates. "I don't have the money to go to any place else," he says. "And you don't have the time . . . This is the biggest and the best cancer center in the whole northwest. Dr. Gillman's the head of it. At least, this part of it. She's got to know something. We've got to trust her, baby. And each other. Ninety-nine percent of this scene is trust."

I know Sam's right. And I do trust Dr. Gillman.

There is no other answer, there is no other doctor, the world over probably, with anything else to say.

Sam takes Jill who is fast asleep and puts her in her crib. What a crazy family life, the three of us here. He reaches over and kisses me, holds me. I can feel his heart beating. He looks at me. "*Now* tell me to leave."

"Leave," I say teasingly, smiling.

"And mean it."

I bury my face up against him. "I couldn't ... Not in a million years."

He kisses me again, then leans back. "Whew ... We'd better be careful, I guess."

"Dr. Gillman'll be back any second," I say.

"I'm going to find us a place," he says. "You'll be out of here soon, then—"

I just look at him, wanting him, but not so it tears me up. We'll have time together, Sam is right.

He's over by the window, looking out. "Oh, by the way, the divorce papers were in the mail this morning." Very casual.

I let out a yelp. "Wow! Where's the champagne?" I start to laugh, I feel so great. Freedom!

"I'm saving it for the wedding," Sam says.

There's a long pause.

"Sure, in the great hereafter?"

"Tomorrow," he says, straight. "After your first treatment."

Is he joking? He wouldn't, would he? Sam is so funny, I can't figure him out. "My mother used to get us milk shakes after the dentist," I say.

"This is for *real*," he says.

I swallow. "We're going to get married? In the hospital?"

Suddenly Sam looks all excited. "Weaver and I met this guy playing at the audition. He studied to be a rabbi once ... Want to be married by an almost-rabbi?"

I give a hoot. "My mother will flip out!"

"He's a hundred feet tall and he looks like Moses," Sam says, pleased with himself. "Except his beard's shorter. He'll keep me humble."

I can't quite believe it somehow, it doesn't seem possible. "Sam, you're serious? ... Is it legal?"

He just grins. "Probably not ... I'll have a justice of the peace waiting in the wings."

I just look at him, puzzled. I don't want to spoil it, but. "Why now?" I say. "I mean, marrying me's like betting on a three-legged horse. You can't win."

He smiles at me. "Sure you can ... If you have a thing for three-legged horses."

I have to cry, I can't help it. I'm too happy.

David and I were married in City Hall. I was wearing a new dress. It was white, but not fancy, I still have it, I like it. I guess there was a feeling of nervousness about it, knowing my parents didn't approve, and a feeling of anger on my part toward them, like they couldn't stop me, no matter what they thought about it. Pat wanted to come. She was the only one who thought it was great. At night she'd come in my room and I'd tell her all the things about where we would live and what a great housekeeper I would be. I liked telling her because she'd look at me with her big, big eyes. She thought I was wonderful and the whole thing was so exciting and David so handsome.

Actually, I got to know David because of Pat. He was supervising at the ice skating rink and she noticed him and dragged me down to see him. I'm a real good ice skater, I've done it since I was five. I thought he was kind of cute and I got out on the ice and started showing off a little, twirling around in my little red skirt.

Well, I was sixteen, what can you expect. He was watching me, I could tell, even though he was supposedly keeping an eye on the little kids, seeing they didn't get into trouble. Only then I fell! I guess I was being a little too much of a show off for my own good because I twisted around and fell kerplunk, right on my bottom. I couldn't look at him, I knew he'd be smiling. I just got up and tried to skate gracefully off the ice. And when I was sitting there, feeling my foot to see if it was okay, he came over and sat down next to me and we started to talk.

If I hadn't met David, I wouldn't have left home, and if I hadn't left home, I wouldn't have met Sam. So maybe all those things are tied together in some crazy way. To say nothing of the fact that if I hadn't married David, I wouldn't've had Jill. So I've been kind of lucky when you think about it. I haven't been mistreated or anything.

If I had to be sick, I'm glad I'm here and I'm glad Dr. Gillman is my doctor. I'm so glad we didn't stay in that hospital in Spokane.

Maybe once I get out of here I'll start trying to write poetry again. I'd like to, if I can. I'm not good. Only once or twice I did a few things I liked, but I still like to do it, try and put in a poem how I feel. I really respect people like Bob Dylan and Leonard Cohen who write such beautiful lyrics. In high school I used to write down poems or songs I really liked. Maybe I'll do that again. Get me a nice, fresh notebook. It would be nice to have really pretty handwriting—mine is kind of sloppy. There was this teacher in our school who knew how to write in a special way with special pens and brushes. I would've liked to learn how from her.

I'm getting married again! Sam is going to be my husband. How weird. It's hard to believe.

As the early dawn comes
and i watch your warm body
rise and fall
in soft slumber
i know
your dreams of today must fade
for today
it will be no better
than before.

Life has brought us to a place
on an old dirt road
in the mountains
and left us with no gasoline for our car.

We must do the best we can
with what has been given us
and live the best we can
for life is real
and can hurt us if we don't.

Givits, the rabbi Sam met at the audition, is really something. Real tall like Sam said, he comes into the hospital room in a crash helmet, a ratty, black shirt, jeans, a fringed vest, gold rimmed glasses, and a wild beard. Wow, my mother would love him. All her fears about her hippy daughter would be proven in one shot if she ever saw him. Only she won't.

Sam looks beautiful. Can you say that of a man? He does. He has this great shirt he must have bought somewhere, a Mexican shirt. He's washed his hair—it's kind of sticking up the way it does just after he's washed it. I know Sam so well, maybe that's why it seems funny that we're getting married. I never knew David at all, even after we'd been married, as well as I know Sam right this minute.

I washed my hair too. I think I still look pretty. I'm thinner, but it makes my eyes look big. Sam brought some flowers for me to wear in my hair.

It's all so crazy! Jill's asleep in her crib and Dr. Gillman and all the doctors and nurses are crowded into the room. I bet none of them ever saw this before, a wedding in a hospital. Weaver, in his usual stuff, is strumming on his guitar.

Givits takes my hand and Sam's and says, in this very soft voice—"Put the ring on her right index finger."

Sam is really nervous! I can tell because his hands are ice cold. He fumbles around for the ring and puts it on my finger. I feel nervous too. I can't look at him. Givits takes the ring off and gives it back to Sam. "Hey, wrong finger!" he says. To me he says, smiling, "Beautiful women always fall for dumb men, why is that?"

Sam puts it on the right finger, I didn't even know!

"Now, you, Kate . . . You put it on Sam."

I do.

Givits grins. "Great, you're getting the hang of it . . . Now, pay attention to this part, folks. We're getting to the crux, the heart, the soul, the foundation." He looks up at Weaver. "Hey, quiet, okay?" Weaver stops strumming. Givits says, "Repeat after me: Behold, thou art consecrated unto me by this ring."

Sam looks right at me. "Behold, thou art consecrated unto me by this ring."

Givits raises his hand. "Note—consecrated means she becomes holy, an object of reverence and utmost regard. Heavy stuff . . . Okay, time to drink."

We pass the wine glass around and each takes a sip. Weaver begins playing again, but softly.

Givits, in a kind of singing chant, says, "Blessed art Thou, O Lord God, who created joy and gladness, bridegroom and bride, mirth and exultation, pleasure and delight, love, brotherhood, peace and fellowship." He takes the glass and drains it, then puts it on the floor in front of Sam. "Step on it," he says; "Smash it."

Sam smashes it. Jill, hearing the sound, stirs in her crib. She sits up, looking at this whole crowd. I can see it from her eyes—who are all these people? Why are my Mommy and Daddy in these funny clothes? Her face is all puckered up, trying to understand.

"Note," Givits says. "As impossible as it would be to put this glass back together, so it is impossible for you to live apart from one another."

Jill begins to cry.

Sam reaches over and hands her to me. I'm glad she's a part of our wedding. I hold her and she quiets down, hanging on to me, looking with big eyes at Givits. He rumples her hair, what little she has. "You almost missed the whole show, sleepy head," he says.

Then he begins singing again, "Banish, Oh Lord,

both grief and wrath, and then the dumb shall exult in song. With the sanction of those present, we will bless our God, in whose abode is joy, and of whose bounty we have partaken . . . Repeat after me—Blessed be our God—"

"Blessed be our God."

"In whose abode is joy," Givits says.

"In whose abode is joy," we all say except Jill who just stares at this funny man with her big eyes.

"Of whose bounty we have partaken."

"Of whose bounty we have partaken."

"Through whose goodness we live."

Sam takes my hand and we look at each other. I know I'm going to cry in one second, but luckily just then he kisses me and my tears brush off on his shirt. Then there's a lot of laughing and noise and Jill, with an indignant yelp, seeing us all sipping champagne, decides it's time for her bottle.

ﻼﻼﻼ

While I'm in the hospital, Sam gets us an apartment. I'll be going in for treatments off and on so he tries to find one not too far away. Finally, one day, Monday, we all drive up to it—it's a small house with three stories. Jill is trying to walk—she's not a year yet, but you can see she's really determined. Mom said I was an early walker and she never knew what to do with me, I got into everything. Well, let her get into whatever she wants. I don't mind.

"Welcome home, Mama," Sam says.

I limp after him on my crutch. I'm getting used to it, I can manage pretty well with it now. "Which one is it?"

"The bay window that hasn't been washed in thirty-five years."

"Oh Sam!" I can't help being excited. Just to be out of the hospital, to have our own place again, not to be surrounded every second by doctors and nurses and sick people.

Sam goes ahead, pointing things out. "Indoor plumbing, not too many steps. Close enough to the hospital to walk when you're feeling stronger, and the whole beautiful world out your window."

I kiss him, laughing. I feel so good, so free. I walk around slowly inside. Sam has set the mattress of our bed on the floor and even tried to make the bed a little, sort of dragged a quilt over it. There's a rocker, some chairs. On the wall some posters. All the stuff from our first apartment. Sam drove down and brought it all up here. It makes me feel good to see our old stuff, though it's not so very beautiful, but I have such good associations with it, with the rocker, with that bed, all the love that started in it. I don't think, even if we got rich one day, I'd ever want to get a new bed.

"It's enormous," I say. "How can we ever afford it? We—"

"Let me worry about that," Sam says. He looks so pleased at having found it, at having set it all up, that I decide not to worry about the money thing just yet.

Even the kitchen isn't bad, though it's small. Lots of cabinets. I think I'll make some curtains, something cheerful in a print. I can pick up some material at the dime store. "I'm going to make a rug," I say. "My grandmother taught me years ago. A rag rug. They're really easy. Then a giant patchwork quilt—"

Jill is running around from room to room with her funny, wide-leg walk. She falls every few steps, but she's so pleased with herself. Sam grabs her and they roll around, she giggling her head off. I love watching them together.

The door opens. It's some girl carrying a pot. She's kind of pretty, but messy, sort of long-haired with a skirt like a gypsy's, earth-motherish. Who's she?

"I thought you children might like something to eat,"

she says. She has one of those throaty voices. "It's chicken and herbs, the baby'll love it. I'm Nora. I live in the basement ... Anytime you want to go out or anything, leave Jill with me, I adore children." She heads out and then calls over her shoulder, "Hammer on the floor if you need anything!"

I look at Sam. I mean, not that I'm the jealous type, but still! "Friend of yours?" I ask mockingly.

He just grins. "She lives downstairs, works in one of those psychedelic shops, I think ... And on the third floor there's a family of Roumanians with a trampoline ... They run a gym or something. You're going to love it."

I feel so tired all of a sudden. I sit down on the bed. Wow, I hope I get some of my energy back. I really do want to do something around here, not just lie in bed all day. Maybe it's the excitement of it being the first day home.

Anyhow, Nora seemed nice. It'll be good to have someone in case we want to go out at night.

Sam looks worried, seeing me lying on the bed. "Want a glass of water?" he says.

I look at him and smile. "Just play me something."

He goes and gets his guitar. Jill lies next to me and we both listen. The sun is streaming in the window. I have a home again.

PART TWO

In the chill of the damp night,
I ran silently and swiftly
to reach my destination,
Thinking as I went,
of the despair and regret
we must face
At tomorrow's departure.
It is strange
that after so short a time
We must return to ourselves
To our own minds,
and decisions.
Why must we face this?
Why must we be forced down again
into the space
from which we've just emerged?
As I reach your door,
I hesitate.
Will this be the last time?
The last happiness we will know?
Perhaps years will pass,
and yet, we are forced to accept it,
For we are not yet old enough
for minds of our own.
Finally in your arms,
I realize,
This isn't the end!
It is only the beginning
The youth of our love,
and happiness.
only our first departure.

᎒᎒᎒

I'm getting used to Vancouver, to living here, to the hospital. When I had the radiation I had to go every day, but that was only for a month or so. Now I just go in every couple of days for my shots. I'm getting to look like a junkie, my arms are all filled with needle jabs in my veins. My leg hurts, but I can forget about it a lot of the time and I'm used to the crutches.

Last week, we went to Sam's parents to pick up Jill. She stayed with them during the time when I was first out of the hospital, when I was getting my strength back. I hated going back to Riverdale to get her. I hated it because it hurt me to be reminded of when I was normal. It made me feel sorry for myself and I don't like that at all.

I like Sam's mother, but I also dislike her. She's so concerned about what people will think of her! She worries about the dumbest things. I almost can't take being around her at times.

Sam is so strong, so sure of his own thing. I love him so much. Last night he cried during the night for me. It's the first time he's let his emotions show, about my disease, so strongly. I felt close like we used to be, before all this happened. He is so wonderful. So much of a man. I love him.

Yes, I love thee
man
Yes supply me with
hope
Yes, I love thee
man
You give me new life.

I'm writing my poems down now in a little note-book. I write them at night or when Jill's napping. I'd like to have a little book of poems to leave her, not just mine which aren't very good, I know, but ones by other people that mean something special to me.

In the end, after we were about a weekend at Sam's parents, I just felt I couldn't take it anymore, the strain was just too damn much. I don't hate Sam's parents, but they sure do make it hard not to. Thelma, his mother, still feels Sam is her little boy and incapable of taking care of himself. Thus, since I married him, I am not capable of caring for either myself or Sam or, most of all, Jill. There are several things I have repeatedly asked her not to do with Jill, yet when I turn my back, she does them. She's this odd mixture of stupid strictness and spoiling. I don't think Jill likes it, it gets her all mixed up.

An example: Thelma is convinced Jill should be off her bottle now that she's over a year. I don't see why, and I told her the baby doctor said he didn't agree, that as long as she wasn't going to sleep sucking on the nipple which might do harm to her teeth, there's nothing wrong with a bottle. He even laughed, saying, "By the time she's married, no one will remember when she stopped her bottle." The time Jill usually wants her bottle is a very reasonable time, to me, around late afternoon, four or five, the time when it's not quite time to begin supper, but it's getting dark out. Lots of grownups have a drink then for the same reason. She'll keep on playing, with the bottle drooping out of her mouth so she can have her hands free. Or she'll set it beside her and now and then throw back her head and take a swig. What I like best are those times she comes to me and says she wants to lie in my lap. It comes out more like "yie in yap" since her l's aren't too clear. She lies down with her head in my lap, drinking her bottle. She keeps her eyes open and drinks seriously and steadily, taking the nipple out just to catch her breath. I stroke her hair which is finally growing in, so soft and fine, and we smile at each other. I see her mouth curve in a smile around her bottle and she holds onto my hand. I guess we must look like some pair of star-crossed lovers from a Hollywood musical. We don't talk at those times, but we're so close.

With Thelma, what bothers me is that because she helps us out financially, she feels she can do as she pleases. So when Jill asks for a bottle, she says, "Now big girls don't do that!" Sort of shaming her, which I hate. Or something like, "You must be a little baby, not a great big grown up girl to want a bottle!" Ugh! I've even asked her to stop giving us money, but she won't. What can I do? What is going to happen when I die? She's not going to have Jill, that's for sure. Sam will just have to understand that. She simply doesn't realize what's good for Jill and what isn't. Her argument is that she has already raised a son, but I don't know just how good a job she did. Right now I am totally mad at Sam and his faults are sticking out like a bad thumb. I love him, despite them. I respect him because he sticks up for them and hates me because I dislike them. But I won't change. His mom is too something or other—fucked up—to raise my daughter.

It's Sunday today, a day of rest. It's so beautiful. It must be fifty-five degrees, I can't believe it. Jill and I sat out on the step this morning. She didn't know what to do! She's just begun to be able to have some freedom outside and doesn't know which way to step first.

She and I have finally developed a good mother-daughter relationship. Since I got sick, things have been a little rough on her. For awhile, after she was with Sam's parents, she was funny and awkward with me. Now she comes to me when she hurts or when strangers are about and we have learned to communicate through touch and sounds that she makes. Everyone has told me, "When they get that age, watch out!" I don't understand. She minds well and is so inquisitive. I hope she is always that way. I'm so happy to see my child be healthy and happy and free and to not worry about a thing. She is a good child. Brag on, proud mama!

Friday, a boy I knew a little at the hospital, Jimmy—he had the same kind of cancer I do—died.

He was sixteen. I felt so down, I can't even think about it. They had amputated his leg, but I guess it didn't help. I try not to think of him and suddenly, just while I'm sitting here with Jill or making supper, I think of it. I better try to pull out of it, I guess.

I have something to look forward to. This coming weekend, Pat, my little sister, is coming up to visit us! I'm so excited to see her again. I haven't seen her for four years. She was twelve then, a kid. Now she'll be grown up. I bet Mom didn't want her to come. She still has this idea that Sam and I are living some wild, hippy existence here. If only she knew! Pat never had too much independence when she was little, but maybe she's changing now. I hope!

"Jill is so cute," Pat says. "She looks just like you, Kate!"

"Do you think so?" I feel so pleased I could burst. "I think she's more like David."

"Well, in coloring, maybe . . . But those big brown eyes, they remind me of you."

Pat is so pretty now, but she still has that sad quality she had when she was little. She's wearing contact lenses. She has that way of talking really low so you have to bend forward to hear her, and a sort of wistful expression. As kids we were close. She used to steal Mom's fall and wear it and tell everyone she was me.

I'm so glad she's come down. She's good for me. I feel a hundred times better since she came. When I heard about Jimmy, I guess it made me feel worse than I really thought I did. I had a sort of sick feeling all the time till Pat came. She's made me get into my old self again.

When Jimmy died, it seemed so cruel. It made me

hate my disease with a new vigor. I can understand about myself, but not anyone else. I've learned a lot about life and love and happiness. I hope Jimmy did too, but most of all I hope his family did.

The other night, when I started thinking about dying, I had the most incredible melancholy feeling. I think that with the thought that I was dying and all, I began speeding a little, but I still felt this incredible calm. All the thoughts of what I should be doing, instead of lying there, were going so fast through my mind I couldn't keep up with them. I kept thinking: let me have time to get everything done. I think I was almost pleading. There's so much I still have to do.

Sometimes, I wonder if I really accept that I am going to die. I thought so until I went to the conference with the doctors at the hospital the other day. They, of course, ask all these questions about death, and dying. How weird! And that always opens up all my thoughts on how I feel and I have to review them. I think I have accepted death, as well as anyone can, but what makes it hard is when I try to talk to people close to me and tell them what I'd like done—with Jill and Sam and my things. They refuse to listen and then I feel funny. It's such a hassle.

I can see all those questions in Pat's eyes, the way she looks at my crutches. She wants to know, but doesn't. I don't think I'll tell her. It would just be putting a burden on her and she's too young for that.

It's after supper and we're in the bedroom. We're going to a dance tonight with Sam and a friend of his, Gene.

"Isn't Jill sweet, really?" I say. "I mean, I know all mothers say that, but she's so good. They always say babies are so egotistical, that they can't think of other people, but she's not like that . . . If I'm tired, sometimes she'll go over and bring this blanket to me and tuck me in ... I guess she likes pretending she's the mommy and I'm the baby. She'll offer me a drink from her bottle even ... Or like with my crutches, sometimes she tries to walk on one leg like me. Or she'll cry when she sees the crutches, like she knows something is wrong."

Pat is frowning, looking at me with a worried expression. "Does she know anything is wrong?"

"No, not really ... Maybe she senses a little. I'm sort of glad she's too young to—"

Pat is fiddling with something. "Are you used to the crutches?" she says.

"Oh sure ... I don't think about them that much," I say. I know I'm not being honest.

"Does your leg hurt you a lot?"

"Sometimes ... It's—well, what bothers me more is the medication they give me. It didn't seem to bother me at first, but lately I get so sick from it."

"You mean like throwing up?"

I nod. "Remember how we used to throw up when we were little and Mom always brought that basin so we wouldn't do it on the floor?"

Pat smiles. "I hated that, I hated throwing up."

"I guess maybe it'll pass, this thing of feeling queasy ... I hope it does."

"You look nice," she says eagerly.

"Yeah, well, at least I'm not fat anymore ... You should have seen me right after Jill was born. I was a hippo!"

"I can't imagine it ... You?"

"Really ... I just ate and ate. Peanut brittle and lollipops, pizza, everything ... If I had another baby, I'd never—" I stop. What's wrong with me? I'm not going to have another baby.

Pat is looking at herself in the mirror with that careful, critical look of a sixteen year old, wanting, praying she'll pass muster. "What do you think about my hair?" she says.

"It's really pretty, Pat . . . It looks nice long."

"Hey girls!" Sam calls. "Aren't you ready yet?"

"Just a sec!" I yell. I like sitting in the bedroom with Pat. It's like the old days.

"Sam is nice," Pat says, sort of shyly.

"Isn't he great? He really is the way he seems. He—" Oh, it's impossible to talk about someone you love. Either it sounds like boasting or as if you're making it up.

"I think he's better for you than David was," Pat says. She giggles. "I was always sort of scared of David."

"Yeah, he was like that." Gosh, David seems so long ago. "I saw him a few months ago."

"Did you? How come?"

"Oh, he tried to pull this thing . . . He said he wanted Jill."

"How could he? She's your baby!"

"I know . . . Only she's his too, technically . . . He didn't want her, it was just to spite me. He said I was too young to be a good mother, all that stuff."

"*I* think you're a wonderful mother," Pat says. "If I ever have a baby I want to be just like you."

No one is like Pat. No one ever just plain admired me the way she does. It makes me feel so good. I can't help saying, "I wish Mom would come see Jill, though . . . I mean, how come she doesn't even care? It's her own grandchild." Oh, quiet, Kate. I know the answer to that, but it just spilled out.

Pat looks embarrassed. She doesn't want to bad-mouth about Mom but she's on my side too which makes it hard for her. "Well, she . . ."

"No, I know," I say bitterly. "I'm her wild, hippy daughter who's living in rags and smoking pot all the time and . . . But if she'd only come down and see! She'd see all that wasn't true! You'll tell her, won't you?"

"Sure," Pat says quickly. But Pat is so meek and gentle. Nothing she says will influence Mom. Somehow, Mom will just think I brainwashed her.

We drive to the dance. Sam is all dressed up in his flowered shirt and looks great. I like Gene, though I don't know him too well. He's small, not much taller than Pat with a kind of scraggly, black moustache and wire glasses. I think he likes Pat which pleases me.

Of course I can't dance! It isn't that I thought I could, but sitting here for three hours watching is more depressing than I thought it would be. It's not just jealousy. I like Sam to dance, I like watching him. I know he loves me, but I know he likes women and he's appealing to them. He ought to dance, it's good for him. And I like watching Pat too. But at the same time it really makes me hurt, makes me want to cry. I don't think that's silly. I love to dance and I think it's a shame that I can't. Damn damn damn! Well, I guess I'll have to find a way to cope. What I hate is when I have to get up to go to the toilet, and all these guys make smart remarks. I just tell them I got hit by a car. That shuts them up. It's not that I'm bitter. If someone asks nicely and with genuine feeling, not with just a desire to hear the gory details, then I tell them the truth. But I hate those dudes that aren't considerate enough to even get out of my way until I've given them a bunch of shit. Gets to be such a drag and it makes me even more self-conscious.

Pat's still here. She'll stay one more day. I'm loving having her, it's like a birthday and Christmas present rolled into one. She's so nice with Jill. If only she weren't so young, then maybe she could be someone to think of to look after Jill after I die.

Tonight they're going to the dance without me. They just left. I guess I'm a coward. I couldn't face it again. That and I felt tired. It's raining out, a good time to curl up in bed and listen to music on the radio, maybe write something in my notebook. They're playing some good stuff, oldies but goodies. Wish they'd play *Sweet Little Sheila*.

Night time is overtaking me
as daylight falls behind.
My life is slowly losing
the sparkle and the shine.
A life filled with promises
and empty bottles of wine.
This loneliness is beginning to
encloak me,
I've lost all sense of time.
Self-pity overwhelms me,
I've begun to lose my mind.
While death is overtaking me
and daylight falls behind.

Sometimes I think I'm very much afraid to be alone. Knowing that I will die makes me want all the life right now that I can get. I don't want to be alone yet.

Being alone in the apartment at night is a little spooky. I'm glad Jill is here. Even if she's asleep, just having her here makes me feel better. I could go down and ask Nora to come up and keep me company. But I don't really like her so much. Ironically, I feel about her what Mom probably feels about me—that she's messy and her life seems haphazard, with no real plan. She knows all these things she doesn't like—she's real down on her family, much worse than me!—but it seems like there isn't so much positive she does like. To me she seems aimless. I don't care if someone works or doesn't work or has a child or doesn't, those are personal decisions, but I do feel people should have something, some center. I see these guys coming to see her and they look grimy. There's no love there, just sleeping around. Wow, I sound like some little old lady. Sermon of the day. Well, I do feel like that, I'm sorry. Maybe being a mama has made me too critical.

When I'm alone like this, every little noise sounds so loud! I hope I'm not getting paranoid.

One thing that's scaring me tonight is that we supposedly have a ghost in the house! All the tenants have heard him and we all thought it was one or the other of us pounding, but then we found it really wasn't any of us! Sam says it's all garbage. He admits there's a noise and he isn't sure what it is, but he's sure it's just some squeaky thing with the house which is pretty old. I don't know. Mrs. Schaeffer, who lives upstairs, told me she thought it was her husband trying to contact her—he died last year. Maybe it's my future ghost calling me to join him! (her!). Oh lordy. I think one does tend to get carried away about such matters. But then, who knows? Perhaps such things do for a fact exist.

"Mommy!" It's Jill. I can't tell if she's asleep or awake. Sometimes she calls out in her sleep.

"What is it, puss?"

She stands up sleepily in her crib. "Morning?"

"No, it's not morning ... It's nighttime. See, how dark it is out."

"Dark," she says, looking around. "Daddy?"

"No, Daddy's not here ... He went to a dance with Aunt Pat ... Are you hungry? Would like a little snack?" I must confess I'm glad she's up. Now I'll have company.

"Jill hungry," she says.

"Okay, let me lift you out."

We decide on bowls of chocolate chip ice cream and some oreos as a snack. She sits next to me on the couch, munching, clearly very pleased to be up. She sees Sam's guitar on the bed. "Mommy play?"

"No, Mommy can't play, darling ... I don't know how."

"Daddy play?"

"Yes, Daddy can play, he's very good."

"Daddy play now?"

"No, Daddy can't play now. He's not here. He's at the dance."

"Dance?"

"You know . . . Jill can dance." I get up and imitate dancing as best I can on one foot.

Jill smiles, delighted. "More dance, Mommy!"

"Well, Mommy's not too good at dancing anymore, puss . . . *You* dance, Jill dance."

She gets up and stumbles around, trying her best, then falls into my lap, giggling. "Puss, you better get back to sleep . . . It's late. It's a long time till morning."

"Mommy sleep?"

"Yes, Mommy will sleep too." I glance at the clock. It's past eleven. I do feel tired. I tuck Jill in her crib and then go and lie down. I see her peeking at me from behind the rails of her crib. "Goodnight, puss."

" 'Night, Mommy."

Soon she is snoring. She sleeps so heavily. I wish I could. Dr. Gillman gave me some pain pills for when my leg bothers me at night, but I hate to take them. They make me so groggy. Anyway, I'd like to be awake when the others get home. But when will that be? Maybe quite late. I lie there, seeing Sam in my mind, dancing.

I do fall asleep, but when they come in I hear them. They must have stopped at the bar again—Sam's breath, as he kisses me, smells of beer. But it's a good smell. I don't mind. Because Pat is here we won't make love, but Sam holds me and that's good enough.

"Was it fun?" I whisper.

"Sort of . . . We missed you."

"Jill woke up . . . But it was nothing. She was just hungry."

"Did the ghost put in an appearance?"

"Come on!"

"Did you have Nora come up?"

"No, I didn't feel like it."

"I just thought you'd like company."

"Umm." I feel petty telling Sam how I feel about Nora so I just say, "I didn't feel lonely . . . I listened to the radio and stuff."

He's stroking my hair. "Sleep tight, sweetheart."

"You too."

Three in the morning. Soon it'll be light. Tomorrow Pat will go home. I'll go to the hospital.

It would be so good if Sam could get a job, a real job, something connected with music that he could really love. Since my illness he's picked up odd jobs here and there, enough so we can scrape by financially without having to mooch too much on his parents. Right now he's bartending at O'Brien's most evenings. But I think having to take that kind of job again bothers him. It's just marking time, and he must feel, as I do, that if it weren't for my illness, maybe I could pull my share somewhat more.

I have to go to the hospital this afternoon. I dread it. The medication is making me so sick. I never feel right anymore. In these couple of months since Pat visited it seems like there hasn't been a day when I haven't thrown up. It's not just that, I feel so—distant, in a fog, like I'm not a real person. It scares the hell out of me.

I can't seem to break out of myself. For days now my thought process has been so dull and I don't know why. I just can't seem to think intelligently. It's really bothering me. Maybe it's the way Sam and I have been living. We're so unaware of what's going on around us. We never read or discuss situations anymore. We just end up arguing about things because we're both too poorly informed to discuss anything. This is a real problem. I think we should do something about it. I think a trip to the library is definitely in order. I've been wanting to go for several days now, but like so many other things we want to do, it hasn't been done. Why? I guess until now it hasn't bothered me quite this much. I wish I could get a job so that I could be out with people. Seclusion is no good at all. I need fresh ideas and new thoughts. My mind has simply used up all of its resources and I have failed to feed it. I think I'll buy some books and put myself on a new diet.

Jill is sleeping. She seems so fussy lately, whining about everything, sucking her thumb. That bothers me too. What can I do?

I'm sitting in the bedroom listening to Sam and Weaver practice. I just wrote an angry poem. Here it is. It's called America Hurrah, Ha, Ha, Ha:

You may take your poverty aid,
and your military aid,
and your foreign aid,
And even your cool aid,
for what it's worth,
america.

You may burn us for
burning our draft cards,
(as our mothers once
burned us before, for
playing with matches.)

but it no longer matters,
america.

You can prosecute us,
for not killing in an unjust war.
for wanting peace.
through a universal, workable understanding,
love.

I don't want to kill a person, for such an unworthy
cause,
as we are fighting for now.

I DEFY YOU AMERICA!

You can imprison us for years,
and months
of young and productive lives
because we happen to have the guts,
america,
the guts,
to stand for what we believe in,
because we are human;
because we retain our humanity,
despite your propaganda.

You can stifle the lives
of those who haven't been told
but not me,
america. I
I'm free, you hear!
They only can understand
as far as you have taught them
(and that's not very far)

their minds have grown lethargic and old.
Freedom can't be won with a song.

Right! It takes many voices
and many songs.
We! We are the ones that matter!
You have grown old
and have done your work.

Let us grow old as we wish.
Step aside.

I prefer the feel of a newborn child,
and a man's hand on my shoulder
to that of a weapon,
whether material,
or immaterial.

I told you I was in a bad mood! Yeah, it's no good,
I know that too. I listen to Sam and Weaver. They
have their music, however good it really is, it's something, their own. It seems I never accomplish anything.
I feel so utterly worthless. A poorly written book of poetry that *no one* will want to read. Even if I *hit* them! I
need to accomplish something and be good at it and be
praised for it. I need an outer source of expression.
Sam always ignores this. When I ask him to read something I've just written, he puts it off till later. I never
am able to get involved in something. There's always
something to do—Sam to feed, Jill to take care of, the
hospital to go to, cancer in the back of my mind, hatred for all the things I am not. And Weaver. Always
the fear that he or his music will take Sam away from
me.

Why did Weaver come up here? And when is he

going to leave? God, I hate a moocher! He's just staying on, thinking we don't mind if he eats our food. Sam had to be an idiot and say that three can eat as cheaply as one. Not when one of them is Weaver!

I guess I should get going now. See you later, folks! Want to bet Weaver is still here when I get back?

The hospital is my second home. I know it so well by now, I know every nurse, every doctor, a lot of the other kids. I don't mind the hospital itself, or the treatments. It's not even the thought of dying I mind the most. Dying is beautiful, even the first time around, at the ripe old age of twenty. It's not easy most of the time, but there is a real beauty to be found in knowing that your end is going to catch up with you faster than you had expected and that you have to get all your loving and laughing and crying done as soon as you can. You know you don't have time to play games. You don't want to waste precious moments doing nothing or feeling nothing.

That's why I mind the medications—because they make the time I do have, however long it may be, meaningless. I want so much to make someone understand that. Each time I come here, I decide I will finally tell Dr. Gillman how I feel. Then I lose courage, knowing she'll be angry at me. But it's *my* life!

When I get out of the hospital, it's raining. Weaver seems to have gone home. Jill is in the kitchen, but I don't have time even to say hi to her. I just rush into the bathroom and vomit into the toilet. I make a wonderful entrance every day like this. Sam is playing his guitar, I'm throwing up. What a great scene. True love.

I lie down on the bed. Oh, I feel so bitter, so down, I can't even fight it. Finally I say, "How can you sing when I'm throwing up?"

"How can you throw up when I'm singing?" Sam says.

"The pills make me throw up!" I scream. "I can't help it. You *know* that."

"The Christians sang when they were thrown to the lions." He smiles. "It just seemed like a good thing to do, in the face of adversity."

I laugh, bitter. I can taste the bitter, sour taste in my mouth from throwing up. As a kid, I liked throwing up because afterward I felt better and I'd eat a bowl of applesauce. Now I feel the same after as before.

Sam gets up and sits on the bed next to me. He touches my hair. I jerk away. I don't want him, I don't want anyone. Shoot me like an old horse. It's better than this. This is torture. "Kate," he says.

"I can't keep my food down," I say, "I can't sleep, my hair is coming out in handfuls and you want me to laugh at your sick jokes . . . I *am* a sick joke."

"Then laugh at yourself."

"I can't!"

"It's better than crying."

I get up. "I'm *not* crying!"

"Baby—"

"They can't even find a vein that's any good any more to put the shots in. They're going to have to put it in my temple next time. Oh, it's a riot. A laugh a minute." I go into the kitchen and there's Jill, in the middle of the most incredible mess. She's gotten out this bottle of ketchup and has smeared it on everything—herself, the wall, the floor. Can't Sam keep an eye on her for one second and put down that damned guitar!

"What are you doing!" I scream, snatching the ketchup bottle from her. "You know better than that. That's bad. You're a bad, bad girl!" I yank her off the kitchen table, but Sam comes in and grabs her away from me. His face! Like I'm going to kill her. I'm her *mother!*

Jill breaks loose and runs into the next room.

"Sam—"

"Let me get Jill," he says curtly.

"Talk to *me!*"

He pulls away, angry. "In a minute!"

He goes off after her and takes her in the bathroom. I can hear the water running. He must be washing her off. I can't help it, I go in the rocker and cry. It's all going, everything I love, I'm killing it, I'm destroying Jill and Sam. There's nothing left. I'm becoming a monster.

Sam comes in with Jill. Now she looks mad, but he looks calm.

"Why don't we go out to the park?" Sam says.

"It's raining."

"It's stopped . . . Look."

"Park! Park!" Jill says, excited.

I look at her, her rumpled hair. My baby. "Come give Mommy a kiss first," I say. "To cheer her up . . . Okay?"

Jill looks at me evenly, as though considering the proposition. Then, "No!" she says stubbornly and loudly. She runs to the door.

"Kate, come on," Sam says. "Come with us."

"I'm not going to any stupid park with a child who hates me."

"She doesn't hate you."

"I'm not going to compete with you for my baby!"

"Nobody's competing."

"She's mine, Sam. Remember? Not yours. You're stealing her from me. The only thing in the world that's altogether mine. I know what you're doing—"

His face is cold, angry again. "Sure, I'm taking care of another man's kid twenty-four hours a day just out of spite. I have nothing else to do."

"You don't have a job."

"How will I get a job if I'm a full-time baby sitter?"

"Then leave her! Leave us! Who said you should do it!"

"I love her. I do it because I love her . . . And I love you when you act like yourself."

"This is myself."

"It's not." He turns and takes Jill's hand.

I call after them, "You're teaching her to hate me so that when I die she won't be so much trouble. You can marry any old broad. Anyone'll be better than mean old Mommy who—"

They're gone. Oh God, maybe they won't come back. I feel like I'm at the bottom of a well. I can't see, I can't hear, I can't move. If Jill turns against me, that's the end. That matters so much to me, loving her, having her love me. If she ever felt about me the way I got to feel about Mom, I would truly die. I know one reason Mom never liked me was because Dad did, I was his favorite. He used to kind of flirt with me and whirl me around and she'd get this real angry, hostile expression. Or if he took me out, just to the zoo or to the candy store, anything, she'd get a sick headache and have to go to bed. If they had a fight, she'd say to me sarcastically, "You ask your father. For you, he'll do it." It wasn't my fault! I didn't make him like me! But I knew she held it against me.

If Jill feels that way—oh God. I'm not jealous of her that way. Sam and I have something good together. I would like nothing better than if she, when she grows up, finds someone as good as Sam. But lately, I feel I have no patience with her. I don't care about the ketchup. So what? So she spills it! It can be cleaned up in a second. I know that. I ever like her to mess around, I want her to, I want her to get dirty and play in the mud. I never want her to be dressed up in some pink, ruffly dress and then spanked because she got it dirty. Let her wear overalls if she's more comfortable in them . . . But I just don't have any patience. What's happened? I just snap like a string.

Maybe I am jealous of both of them. Of Sam for having his music. Even if he doesn't have a job, he has a center to his life, something he's good at, something he loves, something that brings him in contact with others . . . And I feel jealous of Jill because—well, this sounds ironical now—but because she has the freedom I never did, she has parents who let her do what she wants. She'll be strong when she grows up. Maybe I mind that she's too young to know about my sickness. Really, I'm glad. Because why should she have that? It would just be a burden. It would be worse, much worse if she was just old enough to understand, but not to really understand. I feel that, but at times she seems so heartless not to know, to go on doing her own baby things while I'm throwing up and my leg is hurting. For all she knows, that's what all mommies do. All mommies throw up every day. That's just their thing.

I shouldn't have blamed Sam for not looking after

Jill well enough. He does it so well, better than me, he's so much more patient. And I'm not even sure that's just because he's not sick, I think he really is good with kids, really senses their moods very well ... Of course, he can't watch her every second. He does have to practice. How will he get good enough to audition otherwise? ... Anyway, I don't watch Jill every second I'm with her. You'd go crazy if you did that.

Should I go after them? Where did they go, even? There's one park near here. That's where they probably went. Jill likes it because it has this funny climbing thing in the middle painted with all different colors. And it has two slides, a little one for small children and a big one for big children. I usually take her there a few times a week.

Okay, I'll go there. I still feel sick, but maybe getting out would be good.

There they are. I see Sam standing near the bottom of the slide. Jill is at the top, just sitting there, kicking her legs, building up the suspense of when she'll slide down. I stand a minute watching them. Then I go down the hill. I walk slowly over to Sam, my crutch under my arm. "Hi."

He turns. "Hi," he says. He doesn't smile.

"I figured I could use some air."

He just nods, abstracted.

Jill sees me and waves. "Hi, Mommy!"

Jesus, children forget so fast! "Hi, honey! ... Are you sliding down?"

I see another child climbing up behind her. "I'm at the top," she says.

"I see, that's great ... Are you going to come down?"

Finally, reluctantly, feeling the impatient breath of the next child, she lets go and slides to the bottom.

Then she races over to the climbing thing and crawls in. It's filthy and wet from the rain. Okay, let it go. She'll have a bath when she gets home anyway.

"I feel so badly when we fight like that," Sam says.

"I know." I take his hand. It's cold.

"Especially in front of Jill."

"Kids are tougher than we are," I say flippantly.

"I don't know about that."

"She's forgotten already . . . Look at her!" Jill is peeking out of the holes in the climbing bar. She waves at us.

"Should Daddy lift you down?" Sam asks.

"No!" Jill says indignantly. "Do it *myself*!"

He laughs. "Everything is 'do it myself' lately, I guess."

I seem to see us from a distance. A couple holding hands, a pretty little girl, married less than a year, happiness . . . Tomorrow I will go into the hospital and Dr. Gillman will say: There's a new drug, just discovered, with amazing results. No side effects . . . Yeah sure.

Jill climbs down and falls on her bottom, but pulls herself up again. She loves being out of doors. Cold, rainy days she'll stand by the door looking out sadly. You've forgiven me, haven't you, puss?

"Maybe we better get back . . . Jill can have her bath. I got some bubble stuff for her."

"Okay." Sam still seems distant, a little detached. I know our arguing takes a lot out of him also, and that makes me feel bad.

As we're walking off, two men come into the playground with two dogs. Mongrels, probably, but nice-looking ones. They both go right over to the slide—the dogs, that is—climb up the steps and slide down. Jill lets out a delighted laugh. "Did you see, Mommy?"

"Yes . . . Isn't that amazing?"

Then the dogs, on command, leap over the fence surrounding the swings. I watch Jill's face. Will she remember that years from now? I was in the playground with my mommy and daddy and two dogs went down a slide? Or is she too young? Will all this fade? I can't remember anything from when I was her age. That seems so strange, that one would remember nothing. But that's the way it is, I guess. I pray I live long enough to see Jill become a human being independent of Sam and me. At least old enough to reason some on her own. Old enough so she'll remember me.

"We can pick up a pizza on the way home," Sam says. He has his arm around my shoulder, more relaxed again.

"I want a horsie ride!" Jill calls impatiently and he bends down and scoops her up high onto his shoulders. "I'm bigger than you, Mommy."

"I see, puss." The other day Jill and I were playing with two cats, one the mother, the other, now full-grown, the son. I began explaining how one day she would be bigger than me, just like the cat was now bigger than his mother. She seemed to be listening very carefully and then at the end she said, "When I grow up, I will be a pussy cat." I said, "No, when you grow up, you'll be a big woman, like Mommy," but that didn't please her at all. She insisted that she was going to be a pussy cat and nothing I could say would dissuade her.

♥§⧉♥

Jill likes to watch me put on my makeup. "Me ma" she calls it, "Mommy's me ma." It's funny. Before I got sick I hardly wore any—oh, maybe some eye makeup when I wanted to look good because I think my eyes are my best feature. But since I've been sick, I've been wearing lipstick and rouge just so I won't look so pale and wretched. Sam put these photos up in the bathroom. There's one of me before I got sick. I was so much heavier in the cheeks—now my bones are very hollow. I'm very photogenic now, like a model. But to me it's the same face. I see in it the spark of laughter that made me such a happy child and the traces of wisdom that made me a mother. I see the pain and beauty of childbirth, the agony of loss of health, the peace from trying to gain freedom over all of it. I see a woman. I don't look like a girl anymore. I see a few lines, lines of struggle, lines on my nineteen year old face—a map of pain and sorrow and joy and happiness, and perhaps at my eyes and mouth peace in knowing who I am.

"Put lipstick on me, Mommy," Jill says. She purses her lips and I stroke them gently with the tip of the lipstick.

"Put rouge on me." You don't need rouge, you silly. She looks funny with rouge. She won't let me blend it in so it's just two red streaks on her fat cheeks.

Jill's getting pretty. I can tell by the way people look at her and smile. I'm glad. I wouldn't want her to be spectacularly beautiful, like a movie actress, but I think being pretty, nice-looking, makes things easier. She's a baby still, but she's so much into things, so much a part of every moment. She loves to play dress up, draping these old scarves and things around her. Sometimes she'll put on ten at once, like an old gypsy fortune teller. She gets mad when they fall off. When I clean house, she goes around copying me, pretending to dust. In the car she sticks her head out the window and sings to the wind and the passing cars. She only knows one song, "Oh, we're going in the car, oh, we're going in the train, oh, we're going in the boat . . ." It can go on forever, like a chant. Sometimes she tries to walk on one leg like I do. What will she be like when she grows up? Maybe she'll be tall and willowy and sing sad songs or maybe, more likely, she'll be giving songs to people from her heart instead of just singing sad ones.

"Mommy has to go now, puss," I say, having done the best I can with my face.

"Jill go too?"

"No, Jill will stay with Nora . . . Mommy will be back soon and then we'll go to the park."

I know Jill doesn't like staying with Nora. I pray that today she goes off without a fuss. It wears me down so to leave after a huge battle. What else can I do?

"Mommy will see you later," I say as Nora comes out to greet us.

"Don't go, Mommy!" Jill says suddenly. She comes running to me, clutching me around the knees.

"Darling, I have to, I have to go to the hospital."

"Take me . . . I want to go too."

"I can't take you . . . They don't allow little girls."

"Let's play your game, Jill," Nora says in a cheerful voice. She says once I leave Jill's okay.

"No!" Jill yells. "Mommy will stay!"

I yank away from her. "Jill, stop it!" I hear my voice, too shrill, on the verge of hysteria. "Leave me alone!"

"Just go!" Nora says. She holds Jill back by force. Jill's face is red from screaming. She looks like she's going to have a heart attack.

I dash away, not daring to look at them. Oh God, I hate this! Why can't Sam be here when I leave? Once I'm out of sight, my heart still pounding too fast, I wish I hadn't gotten hysterical. I can't help it, lately. I feel myself getting out of control, but I can't stop it. It's awful.

I'm going to tell Dr. Gillman today to take me off the drugs and the radiation. Every night I've been preparing what I'll say to her. It's so important to me that she understand, understand what they've been doing to me. I trust her, more than any of the other doctors. For some of them I think a patient is just a guinea pig. They want to try the medication just to see "how it works." They've trained themselves not to think of their patients as human beings. I can understand that. It must be hard to become attached to people and then have them just die on you. But I think it's so much more important that they consider each patient, how the medication is affecting them. They do these tests on monkeys, or whatever, and then try them out on their patients, not seeming to care that we're not monkeys. That sounds silly to even have to think, but there are many times when I don't think they make any distinction. We're like laboratory animals.

As far as I'm concerned, they can take their egos and go sit on them. My life is important to me and if I'm only going to live a short time, then, that's cool, but I'm going to live it to the fullest.

It's so easy to say this to myself, it all seems so perfectly clear and understandable, but as I try to explain it to Dr. Gillman, I feel myself getting stubborn and defensive, afraid she's going to get angry at me. I need her approval which is childish, I know.

"You don't feel you want to try it a few months more?" she says.

"I've tried it! I've been on it six months! ... Why are you such an egotist?"

She smiled. "In what way am I an egotist?"

"Because if you weren't, you'd see how I feel! You'd say—okay, we tried to help you with these drugs, but if you feel you're unable to take them, then we want to understand why. You'd see that a person's mind is just as important as their body in getting well . . . Maybe for some people the drugs are fine, but you'd say—Kate isn't 'some people'—she's a particular person."

"I *do* want to understand, Kate. Believe me, I do."

"Then understand!"

"It's a matter of prolonging your life—"

"I'm not *alive*! That's what I'm trying to say. With these drugs I don't even want to live. I've lost the will to live, to care for my family. I'm too emotionally upset to look after Jill. I don't pay attention to anything but my own self pity or sorrow. It's horrible!"

Dr. Gillman brings a chair and sits down next to me. She takes my hand in hers. I can tell by her touch that she understands and that makes me so relieved I want to cry. But I can't, I can't talk even. I just sit, so glad for her warmth. Finally, I look up at her. "You ought to find yourself a man and have about two hundred children . . . You'd be the world's greatest mother."

"I have three hundred and fifty children right here . . . You're my oldest."

I look at her, mocking. "And your most difficult?"

"Right now."

There's a long silence. I don't think she did understand, only that I hurt and she senses that. I can tell she still thinks I'm acting like a child, not obeying what she says will be good for me. "I'll give you Jill," I say.

She looks startled. "What do you mean?"

"Either take me off all this stuff—the shots, the pills, the radiation . . . or take Jill. Because it's not fair to her to have a mother who acts the way I do when I'm on this stuff. I can't do it to her."

"That's a bit extreme, don't you think?"

"Look, I could go on with it, maybe, if it just meant throwing up three times a day and flushing my hair out in tufts every day. I'm even getting used to looking like a piece of spaghetti . . . But I'll never get used to what I'm doing to Sam and Jill."

"Sam understands, though, doesn't he?"

"Maybe, some . . . but Jill doesn't. She *can't!* All she knows is that her mommy is screaming at her twenty-five hours a day . . . She never used to cry at all. She didn't have any reason to. She was happy. Now she cries all the time. She cries in her sleep. She wakes up crying. She has nightmares. She chews her fingers. If I come to her in the night, she screams ... The only thing I ever really wanted to do is to have a child, a girl, and raise her like I should've been raised. With nothing but love and freedom. With no fancy clothes and stiff shoes, no Puritan ethic, no rules, no right answers to everything. So she could be open to the sun and snow and rocks and rain and know how to love. It's terribly hard when you've never been loved. When all you've ever known is people screaming at you and telling you you're bad."

My voice is getting shaky, but I feel I've said it all and if she doesn't understand now, she never will.

"If you go off the medication, you will die," Dr. Gillman says.

"I'm going to die anyway."

She hesitates. "Probably, yes."

"So, don't you see, I'd much rather die peacefully with some semblance of sanity than take the drugs and die a bit later than I might have naturally with no mind at all ... That's what's happening to me. I'm losing my mind."

"I see."

"Do you really? ... I mean, tell me if you don't."

"I do."

"Will the other doctors? ... Will I have to go through this again with them? I'm not sure I can."

"I'll speak to them."

I feel wiped out. I can tell my body is wet with sweat under my turtleneck.

"I think Jill is lucky to have a mother who cares that much about relating to her."

I wince a little. "I don't know. I wonder if she's lucky ... Sometimes I think—it's so hard for all of us ... There's so much I would've liked to tell her, do with her, and she's just too young! I can't."

"Have you ever thought of writing it down?"

"Oh, I do . . . poems and things. But I'm not a good poet."

"Well, why don't you write prose, then? Just all those things you were mentioning that you'd like to tell her about?"

"Well . . . I don't know. I don't know if I can . . . Where would I start?

"Anticipate her questions . . . When she's six, what you'd say to her. What she's going to want to know."

"Nothing." I laugh. "By the time you're six, you know everything."

"Then—when she's ten or sixteen, whatever."

I try to think about it. Jill at ten, at sixteen.

"About boys, your feeling for nature, love . . . so she'll know you and how you feel about her."

"But the trouble is, I can't type and writing takes so long . . . Somehow when I sit down with a sheet of paper in front of me, I get all tight. I'm that way with letters even. It seems so—I don't know, final, to write it down."

"Why not tape it, then?"

"What do I buy a tape recorder with? Food stamps?"

Dr. Gillman opens her bottom drawer and takes out a tape recorder. It's marked: "Property of children's hospital. Do not remove." She puts some tapes down next to it. "How about it?"

"Can I take it home with me?"

"Sure, that's the point."

"But it belongs to the hospital."

"That's *my* problem."

I stare at it, fascinated. "Will it be hard to learn, how to work it?"

"Not at all . . . You know, I brought it up because

I'm like you, Kate. I get all stiff when I face a piece of paper. So whenever I have a speech or something to deliver, I just speak it into here. Somehow talking is much easier, less official . . . And what's great is you can erase whatever you don't like. It's really simple to work."

I take the tape recorder and tapes in my lap. I love you, Dr. Gillman, I think that but I can't quite bring myself to say it aloud. I'm sure she knows. She knows everything.

"Kate, I'm not trying to revert to our earlier topic, but—"

"Yes?" I steel myself.

"Well, there is a new drug, one we haven't tried on you yet . . . What would you say to trying it just for a short time? . . . If it has the same effect as the others, then we'll discontinue it."

"Has it been tested yet?"

"The experiments are still running. They've been going two years."

"Is it a depressant?"

"No, but—"

"Does it make you throw up?"

"It doesn't make monkeys throw up."

"Wonderful."

"What do you say then?"

"I don't know . . ."

"It's a long shot. I won't lie to you."

"Do you promise that if I come back to you and say it has the same effect as the other drugs you'll take me off it, no questions asked?"

"I promise."

"Cross your heart and hope to die?"

"Kate!" She laughs.

"I wish you'd been my mother," I blurt out.

"Then you wouldn't have been you."

"True . . . but think how great I would have been, how secure . . . *Will* you have a baby one day?"

Her face gets sad. "I don't know . . . I'm so involved in my work, I'm not sure it would be fair."

I can see that. "I hope sometime you do, though . . . because I think you'd love it."

She smiles. Her expression is much softer, more vulnerable than usual. "I hope I will some day."

I go home excited but peaceful. So glad she understood. That in itself makes me so happy . . . But most of all, I'm so excited about having the tape recorder. I want so much, in what time there is left to me, to leave something for Jill, some record on these tapes that later Sam could have typed into a book. Some part of me. I want to tell her about how I feel. About how I did things. About how important she is to me. Now she's too young to understand. But later, when I'm not around, she'd have something to come to, she could hear my voice, listen. I have so many things to tell about, it's hard to know where to begin!

The earliest thing I can remember was when my mother took us to the zoo for the first time and we were feeding the elephants. I ran out of peanuts and popcorn so I grabbed my white sandals off my feet and threw them in. My sisters thought it was a great idea and wanted to throw in more clothes, but Mom caught us before we could strip down. I may think that was the beginning, but I bet Mom thought it was the beginning of the end. I was four then. How I hated those damn sandals!

I remember my mother. I thought she was the most beautiful mommy in the world. I loved the way she smelled, the way she wore her black hair, the proud way she carried herself. When we walked down the streets of town, even with four, grubby, little girls clinging to her skirts, all the men looked, and I wanted to be just like that. And I was. I knew it because men started falling in love with me when I was only eleven.

They saw in me the same fire and beauty that was in her.

There were things I didn't understand about my Mom and Dad. I still don't. They had bad fights. I remember some Christmases he wasn't there. Did he have other women? I don't know. Once there was a fight and he stormed out. Mom was crying and I came and took her in my arms; I must have been twelve or so. I told her I would always take care of her. We held each other so tight! That was one time we loved each other freely without all the bad things, the tension that I always felt between us . . . They had other fights too. One time the six of us went for a ride in the mountains. We had a brand new Oldsmobile, one of those long black and white ones. They could go ninety miles an hour and so could my Dad. He and Mom got in a fight just as we came to what is known as Five Mile Hill up the Poudre Canyon in Colorado. Dad started up the hill as fast as he could go just to scare Mom. I know he must have been going sixty-five at the time, and that's a lot on a little, dirt road. We girls sat in the back scared stiff, our feet straight out in front of us, and heads back against the seat, fervently praying. But Daddy was a good driver and we made it to the top of the hill!

I know one thing Mom holds against me is the time I got drunk with Henry McDoughall just before I went off and married David. I was just scared about getting married, that was all. Maybe it was my way of showing her I was scared, wanting her to understand and sympathize. I never drank outside of that time. I really can't stand liquor or beer to this day. I never smoked either, not even grass that much because Mom taught me how to get high when she taught me the names of mountain flowers and when she taught me to speak up for myself and when she taught me how to love, when she gave me my first dog. She taught me living was beautiful and I believed her because she was beautiful and knew how to share it. If only I could understand why things got bad between us!

I can't remember too much of school. There were all those games: red rover, red rover, let Kate come over! I didn't like that game. I could never get through and I always got sent back and then no one on my side would let me play again. I had a friend in first grade. Her name was Alice. We pretended to be sisters. Everyone thought we were a little crazy, but we didn't care. We would hide in the top of the fire escape tunnel and whisper stories about our parents to each other. I told her how after we went to bed, my Dad and Mom would sit up and drink beer and kiss and stuff. She said her parents did too.

One day in the lunchroom a little kid bit into a piece of pizza and got a straight pin stuck in his mouth. He screamed and everyone got scared. I went to the girl's lavatory (as we were instructed to call it) and threw up. Mom let me take my lunch to school after that.

On shot days I'd try to be sick and stay home, but Mom knew my tricks and sent me to school anyway. I used to have visions of the needle breaking off in my arm and traveling around in my body until it finally stabbed me in the heart, causing my death. People would come to my funeral and mourn. The school nurses would be thrown out of town and shots would be abolished ... I had asthma too, and was allergic to goldenrod, so that meant more shots. A lovely summer day, sneeze, sneeze. The next thing I knew I'd be in the doctor's office getting shots for asthma. Tall white walls, stainless steel medicine chest, stainless steel nurses. Count to ten, dearie, you won't feel a thing. 1 2 3 Mama, are you still there? 4 5 Please lady, don't let it hurt. 6—jab! Screams would erupt from my body like volcanic explosions. Momma, let's go home and not come here anymore.

We never got an allowance. There just wasn't any extra money to go around, especially with the four of us. If I wanted to earn money, I'd pick pine cones. There was a woman in a nearby village who made Christmas wreaths for people. I gathered the pine cones to put on those wreaths. Eventually, I graduated to tying the wreaths and then to decorating them. But the first thing I did was gather pine cones.

You got a pair of long clippers and gloves and went into the mountains, picking up whatever pine cones you could find that were perfect, very brown and not broken. If there weren't enough on the ground, you had to climb the trees and go out very dangerously to the end of the tallest branches where the cones were. You had to clip off only the cone without damaging the tree. It was very important to me to be careful of the tree so I just clipped the very corners of the ends. Then I would scramble down the tree, twist the cones off the branch and put them into my gunny sack. I tried to gather at least a gunnysackful a day, about five hundred cones. At three cents apiece that was a lot of money. I could buy a dress or a pair of boots or a hat, something I wanted very much that my parents couldn't afford to buy me.

In the early spring and late summer we would pick gooseberries and currants and sell them to grocery markets. We'd have to go out in knee boots so the snakes couldn't bite us, but we weren't afraid. I wonder if country kids still make their money the way we did. Probably. It was a funny life, being a country kid but going to school in a bigger place. It made me feel I had two different lives and they never quite came together.

Life at home was close to nature. It meant doing chores, getting up at six in the morning to milk the cows, chopping wood for the fire, hauling water, feeding the pigs and the baby calves with bottles. Going to school meant being in a place where the girls wore nylons and high heels and mascara. It was hard on us; they used to tease us.

My life has changed so since I got the tape recorder from Dr. Gillman. When Sam is out or Jill is sleeping, I sit down with it and spin out my thoughts. It never talks back! We never have fights. It's a perfect friend! I love it, which may be a crazy thing to say about a machine, but I do. Sam seems jealous of it at times, isn't that funny? I guess before I had the recorder I gave all my attention to him and Jill, and now I have something else. He ought to understand, since music is so important to him, but I'm not sure he does completely.

I feel I really needed the tape recorder. Knowing that I'm off the medication and that I may die sooner than otherwise, it's even more important to me than ever to get these things down in time, before I become too weak or the pain is just too much. So far I'm okay, it's not worse than before. How long that will last I guess no one knows.

Nora is here, helping in the kitchen. I think she's got

a thing for Sam. I see her giving him these glances. Does she need him, really? She must have a dozen lovers, all shapes, sizes, and types. Okay, I'm jealous. But she really has been nice, especially about Jill. Nora, please leave my man alone, that's all I ask!

Givits and Weaver are practicing inside. They want to work up their act with Sam so they can get a job at some night club. I know their songs inside-out by now. Sam is helping clean up after supper. He's good about that. It would be too much for me, with feeding Jill and my leg and all. I'm glad he understands that.

"How're the tapes going?" Nora says.

"It's great," I say. "I love it. It's the most wonderful invention! I almost feel guilty about it."

"Well, anything that makes you so happy can't be bad. Even if it is a machine."

"It's some trip," Sam says, "no two ways about it."

"It's an ego trip, is what it is," Weaver shouts in.

Thanks, pal. Givits says, "What isn't an ego trip? Whatever you dig is an ego trip."

"Even dying," Weaver says.

Nora looks at me. "What's with him?"

In an undertone I say, "He's jealous . . . He thinks I take Sam from his music. He'd like him to rehearse morning, noon, and night."

"Hey, Sam!" Weaver yells. "Let the chicks clean up, will you? We haven't rehearsed in two weeks."

Nora smiles at me. "I see what you mean." She goes into the next room.

I wipe Jill's mouth off. She insists on feeding herself everything, and the result can be kind of a mess.

"Kate," Sam says, sort of low.

I turn around. He's holding the pills Dr. Gillman gave me, the ones she said were a long shot. I haven't taken them for a week. She knows. We talked about it.

"You aren't taking these," Sam says, accusingly.

"They made me sick, just like the others." I hate talking about this with the others right in the next room. "Let's talk about it later."

I turn to go, but he catches my wrist and holds it tight. He's angry. "Let's talk about it *now*."

"I *told* you, they made me sick."

"You didn't give your body time to get used to them. How many did you take? Two? Three?"

"I took them for fifteen lousy days . . . Just stop it!"

"You didn't give the other medication a chance either."

"They made me *sick*! Dammit, is that so hard to understand? These made me dizzy on top of everything else. I fell down. I couldn't take care of Jill. I couldn't think . . . I couldn't even work on my book."

"That damn book is more important to you than living," he says, furious.

"Yes!"

He hurls the bottle of pills into the garbage. "You're out of your head."

"Thanks for being so understanding."

"What about Jill?"

I look at him, feeling torn apart. "It's for Jill I'm doing it!"

"That's some crazy logic."

"It isn't!"

"Hey, Sam!" It's Givits from the other room.

He gives me one long look full of contempt and goes in to the others.

It's time for Jill's nap. I tuck her in and sneak out, not that they'd notice me anyway, they're so absorbed in their music.

Why can't Sam understand about my going off the

medication? It's for him too, that's what's so ironical.
He didn't like the person I was becoming either. Making love was lousy, I lay around, hardly able to stir
myself. Maybe he thought that was just my being sick,
being depressed about it. It wasn't! It was Sam who
said I shouldn't think about dying all the time, that I
should think about living, about all I wanted to do,
about all *we* wanted to do. That's why I did this, because I knew on the medication I'd never *do* any of
those things. And I'd leave behind nothing, nothing for
Jill to remember me. I can't bear that!

About so many other things Sam is understanding.
He's not a cruel or a stupid, thick-headed person. But I
think maybe he's scared. Watching someone die must
be different from dying. Not worse, but different. I
think it's really he who'd like to pretend that it's not
happening, that some miracle cure will come along.
Sure, big chance.

I keep thinking of that movie, *Love Story*, which we
saw awhile back. It makes me angry even thinking of
it. Her husband was so perfect, so kind, and she always
was so lovely—she never even went for medication!
Christ! That's so unrealistic! Movies like that should be
banned, I think. They make the whole thing so unreal,
as though you could die without pain or ugliness. I feel
I'm learning something from all this, but at times I'm
not sure I want to. I'm not sure I want to see these
things in Sam, see his weaknesses. How come *her*
hair didn't fall out? Why didn't she throw up every
day? How come they never argued about anything because they were both scared and angry at the unfairness of it all! Oh, calm down, Kate. Don't go off
ranting. What purpose does that serve? Just get it off
my chest, I guess.

When I get back, Sam isn't there. I go downstairs to

Nora's apartment to get Jill. "When did they go out?" I ask.

"Oh, around five or so."

"Did they say when they'd be back?"

"Uh uh."

I take Jill up to our place. She seems subdued, quiet. "How is my pooch?" I say, holding her.

"I'm not your pooch . . . I'm your ooch," she says. "You're *my* pooch."

"Where did Daddy go?" I say, as though she would know. But I like talking to her, she's a person, she looks at me with interest, understanding.

"Daddy go?" she repeats. "Men go . . . Catar go."

That's how she pronounces guitar, like it was a sickness. Maybe it is. Maybe it's them who are into an ego trip with all their obsession about when they'll make it and what they'll do with all that money. Fuck them!

I read some books to Jill. She turns the pages very fast so I just have to make up some kind of commentary on the action as fast as I can. It's funny—she loves the parts where one of the main characters tries to do or does something anti-social. When the little girl in the story takes out a sharp knife and is reprimanded, Jill's eyes sparkle. "She's bad!" she says excitedly. "She's as bad as Mr. Jones!" Mr. Jones is a tiny peg figure, no bigger than two inches tall with a barely discernible face. Somehow, I forget how, we made up a game where I set him down and say something like, "Now Mr. Jones, you behave yourself. No more wild stuff today. I mean it!" Then I throw Mr. Jones across the room and say, "Mr. Jones, you stop that! What did I tell you?" This goes on with Mr. Jones disobeying all orders to remain in place, and flying all around the room, crashing into things. Jill laughs hysterically; it's her favorite game. Really, she herself isn't so wild.

Maybe because she senses she wouldn't be punished, she doesn't have to bother doing anything naughty. I think a lot of my wildness as a kid was a taunting thing, wanting attention, knowing it would get a rise out of someone.

At midnight or so Sam comes in. I've been lying listening to the radio. Some old Bob Dylan songs which I love. "Hi," I say evenly.

He says nothing.

"Thanks for leaving me a note saying where you were going," I say.

"Oh, cut it out!" he says. He pulls off his clothes and gets into bed beside me. "I'm going to call Dr. Gillman tomorrow," he says.

"Why, is your leg bothering you?"

"I don't seem to have any effect on you, whatever I say . . . Well, maybe she will!"

"Sam, I've talked about it with her! She understands why I don't want to continue the medication."

"Well, I want to hear it from her own mouth."

"Okay, fine, hear it from her own mouth. But why don't you understand?"

He makes love to me, but he's still in an angry mood. He needs someone and I'm here. God, that's ugly, to think it's become like this when it was so good before. I can feel myself respond physically, but there's nothing joyous in it, no love.

Dr. Gillman comes for lunch. She's never been here, never seen our place. Even though it's not the most pleasant of occasions to have her, I feel pleased she's coming. I wash and wax the kitchen floor and dust around. I know she's not like my mother. She won't be disapproving if there's a dirty dish in the sink, but I want her to see things looking nice.

Sam goes in the kitchen to make some sandwiches. I sit in the rocker with Jill on my lap.

"How're the tapes coming?" Dr. Gillman asks.

"Wonderful ... It's the best present anyone ever gave me ... But let me know, like if you need to make a speech—"

She looks startled.

"You know, you said how sometimes you use it when you have to—"

"Oh, right ... No, you keep it for now."

"Mustard on your ham?" Sam calls in.

"Thank you, yes," she says.

"If I can get it all down, no, not all of it, maybe that's impossible, but most of what I want to say to Jill, that's all I care about ... I never could have done it on the drugs. It's weird but I know what it's like to be a drug addict, but in the bad way, I guess I never got any highs from it ... I know I'll die sooner this way, but—"

"Like tomorrow, maybe?" Sam calls from the kitchen.

"I'm not going to die tomorrow!" I yell back. "Do you want me to?"

No answer.

"No, I figure I'll have a couple of months. And that's all I need."

"Sam, it's Kate's decision," Dr. Gillman says to Sam as he comes in and hands her the sandwich.

"It's *not* Kate's decision!" he says. "Look at her—she's playing Camille! Don't you see? She's on a death trip."

"I'm not ... I just dig knowing that I'm a person, that I'm capable of love and all it involves. I'm not afraid to love and I'm not afraid to die."

"Bullshit!"

"I think Kate understands that if she goes off all medication she has no chance of prolonging her life. The cancer will grow very fast."

"How fast is very fast?" I say softly.

Sam turns on me. "How can you *ask* that? That's not the issue! With medication you have a chance to live."

"I don't! . . . If I had even a fifty-fifty chance, I would take it. A fifty-fifty chance to live out a normal life . . . I don't, Sam! I have a 15 percent chance to live five years and on medication those five years will be hell."

"But you'd *be* here, Jill would have you, I'd have you—"

"You wouldn't . . . You'd have a lifeless body, you'd have an ugly, bitchy vegetable . . . I don't want my daughter to remember me that way! I don't want you to!"

"Well, you don't seem all that serene right now."

"I'm not serene because you don't understand. You're fighting me. Dr. Gillman understands and *you* can't!"

Sam looks at both of us. "Look, thirty years ago someone died a day or a week before a cure for diphtheria or pneumonia was discovered . . . Do you want to die a day before they discover a cure for cancer?"

"That's a pipe dream . . . They're not going to discover a cure for cancer in one day."

"Why not? They're working on it . . . Maybe they will."

"I'm afraid I agree with Kate, Sam," Dr. Gillman says. "They are working on it and I feel confident a cure will come. But I'm not sure I'll live to see it, frankly. It's a very complicated thing, cancer."

"But people have breast cancer and live," he says.

"That's different . . . There surgery and radiation actually can remove it . . . But in bone cancer, that doesn't work . . . Look, I think it could happen many ways. Possibly there'll be an inoculation against cancer like there is for polio and other diseases. There are many ways it can be done. But we're too far from a solution right now."

Sam is silent. Thank you, Dr. Gillman. Oh, I wish I were a billionaire and could leave Dr. Gillman everything. Not that she needs money, I wish I were her fairy godmother then and could give her whatever the one thing is she wants most. "How fast will it spread if she's off the medication?" Sam says, subdued.

"There's no way to predict that . . . It lies in wait, as though it were resting. But when it moves, it moves very rapidly, through the blood."

"But till that happens, till it gets to the lung, I'll have some time, won't I?"

"Some time, yes . . . A few months, possibly."

"And I'm not going to feel much worse than I do now, am I?"

"You'll feel much worse at the very end."

"But up till then—"

"Weaker perhaps, your leg will give you more trouble . . ."

I turn to Sam, though I can hardly bear to. "See? I *do* have time, I have enough time."

"Enough time!" He looks disgusted and angry again. "Enough time for what? To be a wife? To be a mother? To experience everything there is to experience?"

"Sam—" Dr. Gillman says. "It's just not that cut and dried. Kate is going to die. Without medication she will die sooner . . . Some people react so adversely to medication that the difference between dying soon and dying sooner has no meaning to them. Perhaps it's bet-

ter to die with purpose and dignity, even if it's
sooner—"

"Okay, maybe it won't do a bit of good to fight it.
But if it were me, I would."

"It's *not* you," she says, staring him down.

That gets him. He's suddenly quiet. "Well, if you
want my opinion, *you* are committing suicide," he says
to me, "and *you*—" he points to Dr. Gillman, "are a
murderer." He grabs his jacket and his guitar and
slams out the door.

Silence.

"He loves dramatic exits," I say wryly.

Dr. Gillman just stands there. "Kate, try to understand what he's going through."

I shrug. "Thank you, though . . . You were wonderful."

She looks concerned. "Will you manage, Kate, if he
doesn't come back?"

"Sure, I'll manage," I say, maybe too quickly.

"You're positive?"

"He'll come back, don't worry . . . He just couldn't
stand it that you got the best of him in the argument."

"I wasn't trying to get the best of him."

"I know . . . Maybe that made it worse."

"You're very honest, Kate."

"I guess I don't have time not to be."

She leaves. I give Jill supper and take her to the
park, go through the motions. But night comes and
morning and night again and no Sam. Maybe she was
right. He won't come back. That seems so irresponsible
in terms of Jill. Doesn't he care about her, even if he
hates me? That really worries me. Who will look after
Jill after I die if Sam doesn't? I've thought about this
before, but I really have to get it straightened out. I
don't like to sit in judgment, but I must make careful

choices for these are the most formative years for Jill.

Sometimes I think Sam and Nora will get together. But Nora doesn't react right to Jill. She's false with her, for one thing, and Jill feels it. I have the feeling that just because Nora had a bad time with her own parents, she would be the same with a child of her own— from lack of a knowledge of what a good family life can be. Also, though this is petty as hell too, I don't like the way she keeps house or does dishes. I've always hated a dirty house. It seems to breed discontent and germs. Sam and I always fight when the house becomes a mess.

Nora isn't a good balance for Sam either. He can be difficult and moody at times, and you have to be willing to sacrifice some things for him. And do things for him. I don't think Nora could be that consistent for him. When he yells I have to be calm. When he's outrageous, I have to agree, then tell him he's wrong at a more convenient time. Things aren't easy sometimes.

Jill is a beautiful little girl who needs a mother and a father to love her. Why can't I? I hurt, damn it. I *hurt*! Let me have my child, you bastards of disease! You thieves of lives! May a water buffalo piss on your clean white sheets! So there. Why? Why? Why?

Time Time Time
See what's become of me
while I sit and think
of my possibilities.

Look around,
grass is high,
it's the springtime
of my life—

I'm gonna die.

Sometimes high
Sometimes low,
feelin' mean
and dirty
I see my face
reflected there
now scarred,
what once was pretty

I'm lonely.

I've been listening to Simon and Garfunkel. God, are they good. I'm going to write all their songs into my book. So that if I have to go into the hospital, I can read them. Some of the verses are so powerful. I really love them.

&8&

I am a prisoner upon my throne
of dying midnight roses
forgotten by the many worlds
I once held as my own.
And my frozen words agree
in a whisper I scarcely hear
that the brilliant colors once my own
have faded in the sun.

From my fallen window I see
the now alien ocean
of tides flowing with love
of waves crashing an emotion
I will never experience again
because the happiness
the joys
the soft summer sunlight
once my own
have faded in the sun.

As I look across
to the city of confusion
watching
as each moment goes
my tears mark the hours that have passed
and a single winging dove
reminds me of the love
the image of my soul
I once held as my own
and even the sun
is faded.

Night time again. Sam's been gone a week. Seven long days. The days are okay. The house seems quiet without his music, but I don't altogether mind that. I mind it some, though. I do miss him. During the day I keep busy with Jill. We go out a lot, now that it's getting warmer. She takes her old, rag doll and pushes it in the swing. With other children she mostly sits quietly and watches them, not quite taking part. Children are strange, though. The other day one little boy suddenly said to his sister or friend or whatever, "I hate that girl!" meaning Jill who had been sitting quietly to one side. Doing nothing to bother him at all! Kids maybe aren't more vicious than adults, but they certainly don't seem the sweet little creatures they're sometimes painted to be. I got so furious. I know I should let Jill fight her own battles. But when that same little boy, later, went over and out of the blue just started to hit her, I snatched him up and yelled, "You stop that this second! I mean it!" I was ready to kill him I was so angry. His mama was this hugely pregnant lady sitting on a bench who sort of waddled over and said lazily, "Peter, you stop that." My heart was beating madly, I was so angry. Then, later, I thought—that was no good. I'm

not going to always be around. She has to learn to fight
back, to be tough. Jesus. Jill, in any case, was quite impressed by the incident. Several times since then she's
said with a big smile, "Mommy hit that boy . . . He was
bad!" I don't like to think that kind of physical vio-
lence is inherent in men and not in women, but, still,
Jill does seem to me gentle, trusting, expecting people
to treat her well. I can't bear the thought that life will
teach her that's wrong!

I let her stay up late on purpose. We watch t.v. and
cuddle up together. Sometimes, she'll lean on my leg
and it will hurt. I guess I wince a little because she
said, "Mommy's leg hurt?" It comes out "heet" because
her r's aren't too good. That's so sensitive in someone
that young, that she senses my pain. But eventually, often when we're watching t.v. or listening to music, she
dozes off and I put her in to sleep.

Then it's night and that's the worst time. I can't
keep my mind from circling around dark thoughts,
much as I try consciously to push them away. Vague
memories invade my mind. I think of the times I've
spent and thought, my anger, humiliation and sometimes despair fight to come again into my mind, to take
control and force me through the sorrows I have gained
power over. It's so hard to sit and relate these thoughts,
even into the tape recorder. My mind continually snaps
back to the fears and doubts, the hope that I will live.

Then I turn and see Jill sleeping or listen for the
phone or a knock at the door. It's easy to be distracted
when my mind weighs so heavily with thoughts of leaving it all behind.

I think of that time when we first came to Vancouver, when Jill was just a baby, not yet walking or talking. I remember how my second pill would wear out at

about five in the morning and I would lie awake watching the early grey of dawn creep across the smooth, white hospital walls, touching first the ceiling, then creeping down against the walls like a fugitive not wanting to be seen. In the middle of a small fold-up bed, Sam lay sleeping fitfully, tossing and turning, trying to keep vigil over me, but too exhausted to keep awake even for a few minutes. The lump on my leg hurt. My mind was full of empty questions it seemed no one could answer. It seemed I had some kind of cancer, but what did that mean? Why? Why? Why? Torments crashing against my brain like a huge boom crushing buildings.

The nurse would come in and take my temperature. "Would you like another sleeping pill, dearie?" she would ask, stroking my forehead. "Can't you sleep?"

"No," I'd say, "but it's time to get up soon anyway."

Sam would stir in his sleep. Soon breakfast would be coming down the long, white corridors; steaming scrambled eggs, oatmeal, juice, four pieces of toast. Sam would eat it all because I couldn't stand to. Somewhere along the line, through all the doctors and hospitals I'd been to, I'd lost all appetite. I knew Sam was hating every bite because I wasn't sharing it with him, but anyway it kept him fed.

After breakfast life came to the hospital once more. If only for a little while, it at least broke up the monotony of lying in sterile sheets and looking at sterile walls and being afraid to think anything more than sterile thoughts.

Weekends, Sam and I would walk around the sunlit halls, talking, wishing, pouring out our fears to each other. Sam brought me crayons, paper and a mind puzzle. One day he even brought me a papier-mâché kit to make a statue out of. We filled up all the bed pans we could find with water and proceeded to mix the paste and tear strips of paper to make a statue of one of the nurses, Sue Ellen, but it didn't turn out so well and we had to flush it down my private toilet.

In the chill of the damp night
I run silently, swiftly
to my departure.

I am not yet old enough
For a mind of my own,
For despair and regret.
I am not yet old enough
To be forced down again
Into the space
From which I have only just emerged.

As I reach your door, I hesitate.
Will this be the last time?
The last happiness we will know?

What's it like to die? Sometimes, I think I know. It's cold and hard and so lonely. Everybody tries to be nice. I don't know how to react. I wonder what will happen to all my things when I die. Wonder what to do with my books and all the stuff about the house. I hope Sam will remember to water my plants. I'm sort of afraid about dying. I don't regret not taking the drugs. They made me sick in my mind. I didn't care about my family or myself. Or about trying to live, either. I was dead in spirit. I'm just afraid of not knowing what it's like after you die. I don't know how I'll be towards the end. I have to be strong.

In my soul I somehow feel that all is not lost. Maybe I won't die. Maybe, though, is a very big word. I sound like a child, I guess. And I'm lonely for the warmth of my mother. "Mama, cradle me again." It is so safe as a child. Mama, I hurt! Kiss it and make it better. Oh I wish!

Who is going to cradle my little Jill? My angel. What's to become of you? Perhaps you'll be o.k. but I worry so! People, be kind. She's my baby.

There are so many things I wanted to teach her. About life and the way to live and be happy. So much I wanted to talk about. I wanted to help her grow up to be a fine woman, person. I wanted to do what I could to ease the pain of growing up. I don't know what the world will be like for her. Will she be able to breathe clean air or drink pure spring water in the high, free mountains like I did? Will there be war and hatred to fear? Will there even be a world in which she can have a child of her own? If only I knew!

I wish Sam would come back.

The loneliness of the warm spring wind
reminds me you are gone.
A grey shadow on a distant wall,
marks the time that has passed,
since our departure.

The wind has become my constant companion
fashioning lullabys
that whisper your name.
Singing softly of the love we knew,
I think of you,
on still-lingering winter nights.

A month of nights, a year of days,
how long must we wait,
for our return
to the place we once knew,
where life was love, and freedom was a song?

How long can we last,
in our cells, without windows?
We have been forced apart,
thru no desire of our own.

Oh wind, whisper to me,
can we return,
to life, and reality?
Give me a song,
set my heart free.

In the playground I don't talk to many people. I guess I don't feel like getting close to anyone and then having to tell them my long, sad story. So I kind of sit off by myself or bring a book which I pretend to read. That was easier in the winter when sometimes Jill and I were almost the only ones there. Now more people are coming. Today this very friendly, talkative girl comes right over and sits down next to me. "Which is yours?" she says.

"The little girl ... Her name is Jill."

"Oh, she's cute! ... Mine's the little boy over by the water fountain."

"I don't think it's running."

"Oh, he doesn't care ... He likes to mess around there." She fishes out a big pile of knitting.

"What are you making?"

"A sweater, I guess. The trouble is, I like knitting,

but I hate putting it all together. So I send it to my mother-in-law and she fixes it up."

Jill's nose is running and I get up to wipe it.

"What's wrong with your leg?" the girl says. "By the way, I'm Martha."

"I'm Kate . . . It's . . . I was in a car crash."

"You were? That's really a fantastic coincidence." She yanks up the leg of her blue jeans and points. Her leg is covered with scars which are about half-healed. "That's how I got mine . . . I don't know what I'm going to do when summer comes. I've always looked great in a bathing suit . . . What are *you* going to do?"

"I guess I haven't thought about it too much."

"Was yours your fault? I mean were *you* driving?" Before I can answer she says, "Mine was my fault, that's what's awful about it. I was going too fast and the roads were icy and I skidded and the car burst into flames . . . And *he* was with me." She points to her child.

"Did he get hurt?"

"No, I threw him out of the car . . . It's funny how even in something like that you have presence of mind. Or something. I just threw him out the window and he wasn't hurt at all . . . But my leg was a mess. It's still not so great, but it was awful before. It was just this big mess. I'd just gotten divorced and I was feeling really shitty. I guess it was kind of self-destructive . . . I'm out of all that now. I have boy friends, I have a job, but then I was really a mess."

I glance at Jill who seems to be playing happily. "Listen . . . do you think you could keep an eye on my little girl for about five minutes? I have to make a phone call."

"Sure, take your time."

There's a phone booth on the corner. I glance back at Jill; she still seems fine. But I just stand in the phone booth a long time. Should I call? It seems so demeaning, somehow. But, then, do I have time for all those games, that whole pride thing?

I know Sam is probably at *O'Brien's*, this bar where he, Weaver and Givits have been practicing lately. If he's not, I don't know where he is. I dial the number and it rings seven times. In the middle of the eighth ring Sam's voice says, "Yeah?" He sounds sort of curt, as though he'd been interrupted.

"It's me."

"Hi."

"We've missed you."

There's a moment's pause. "Are you going to take the pills?" he says.

"Jill would love to see you. She—"

"That's not what I asked . . . Just answer the question. You take the pills, I'll come back. It's as easy as that."

"But Dr. Gillman—"

"Fuck Dr. Gillman! I don't want to hear any of that garbage, Kate . . . Will you or won't you, that's all I want to know?"

"You know the answer to that, Sam."

"Well, then you know *my* answer to *your* answer . . . So long."

I stand there, the phone in my hand. The hell with him! And the hell with me for calling. We can manage, Jill and I can do okay. We're not helpless . . . Why are the people I love so wonderfully understanding? With your parents you don't have a choice, but with men you do, unless you're horribly ugly or strange or something. I had a choice. Did I pick wrong two times? But Sam seemed so different from David, so kind. If I had

had to list half a dozen adjectives to describe Sam, kind would have been one of the first. I remember this poem I wrote about him once:

Soft as a pressed rose's petal
to touch
is your skin

And dark
as evenings baked in velvet,
your hair.

fiery,
your breath
as it scorches my back

and gentle
your hands
as they touch my breast

I love
you,
your kindness,
my lord.

So, I'm a rotten judge of character, I guess . . . I go back slowly to the playground. Martha is getting ready to leave. She's nice, but a little nutty. I'm glad she's leaving because I don't much feel like talking to anyone. Here I sit, feeling lousy because of Sam and probably half the girls, women in this park have some such trouble. Does that make me feel better? No! Next to me is an elderly lady who beams at Jill. "I bet her grandma spoils her!" she says, winking at me.

"Her grandmother's never seen her," I say, meanly. Oh, stop it, Kate! What has that old lady ever done to you? Is it her fault you pick the wrong men and the wrong parents?

Sitting here, I let myself feel immersed in self-pity. I like to sometimes. Like right now because I'm alone. Because I'm dying. I like being a martyr. At least it gives me something to be.

I start having a fantasy. It's my old constant worry—about Jill, what will happen to her. I imagine that in this park I meet a woman who has one child, but can't have anymore. She's desperate for another child, but it's so hard to adopt, she doesn't know what to do. I see her with her own child and she is lovely, a wonderful mother, kind, gentle, caring. I go over and say: will you take my child after I die? She is delighted, can't believe her good fortune. We smile, Jill seems to like her . . .

Okay, time to go home. End of fantasy.

"Jill, let's go to the plant store, okay, hon?" She trails after me very slowly, pulling a stick behind her.

At the plant store I buy a big pot of ivy. I love having plants around the house. I think it makes the air smell nicer. I lug it home and Jill comes with me while I find a saucer, fill it with water, and put the plant and saucer in the middle of the bay window.

"Ivy grows like mad, Jill, you'll see," I say. "We'll put strings for it to grow on up the sides of the window and across the top. It'll be like a leafy frame. It'll be beautiful."

"I'm wet," Jill says, unimpressed.

"Get me a Pamper, then, okay?"

She trots off and comes back with one. Then she flops down on the bed in the right position. I lean over and kiss her belly button and all around it. "What is this round, fat belly?" I say, nuzzling her. She smiles, indulgently, sleepily. Her lids are heavy; it's past her nap time. By the time I get the Pamper fastened, she's snoring away. I pull the cover over her. The plant does look nice, I'm glad we got it.

In the evening, after supper Nora drops up. "Is this an okay time?"

"Sure."

"I thought Sam might be practicing or something."

I shake my head. "I mean he may be, but not here ... He's sort of—cleared out."

She stares at me. "For good?"

"Evidently."

"The bastard! How could he? How rotten! ... Jesus, I thought you two seemed so happy. You're the only happy couple I've ever seen."

I shrug.

"How do you like that? Wow, men are something, aren't they!"

I like talking to other women, but I've never liked that kind of general "aren't men awful" type of conversation. It seems so general; it never helps.

Nora flops onto the bed. She's wearing some crazy getup, looks a little like Jill when she's doing her gypsy mama bit. "Well, I had a fight with my guy yesterday, but we never—it wasn't like you and Sam."

"Which guy was that?"

"Willie, the black guy . . . You saw him that time, didn't you?"

"Oh yeah, I think so."

"Look, nobody's happy," she says, "so why should *we* be? Why should we be exceptions? My parents hated each other's guts for forty years."

"Mine didn't," I say.

She looks surprised. "Didn't they?"

"No, they loved each other . . . They still do, I think."

"I thought you said your mother was a bitch."

"Well, we don't get along, but . . ."

"Well, my mother, *no* one could have liked, much less loved . . . She was crazy, God rest her whatever. I mean, you know, not like a little off, but the kind that should have been locked up in a padded cell."

I envy Nora in some ways her unequivocal hatred of her mother. If I didn't love Mom it would be a thousand times easier.

"Nora." I look away. "Nora, I'm kind of tired . . . Jill and I were out all day . . . would you mind if I—"

"Oh, go on, go to sleep . . . I have some stuff to do. I just wanted to say hi, see how things were."

After she leaves, I just lie there. The nighttime blues are settling over me. I wish I had a piano. I could play lullabies for Jill. Nora's nice, people have been nice, but there isn't anybody I can cry with. Nobody to touch me. Nobody to say it's okay. Nobody to comfort me and listen to my self-pity. I'm so tied up inside it hurts . . . I wish Pat could come down again.

Maybe I'll call home. If Pat's there, I'll ask her to come down. I have enough money for her ticket.

"Hi, Mom, I hope it isn't too late to call."

"Well, your father is in bed . . . I was just doing some things . . ."

"How are you?"

"Oh, as well as can be expected, I guess . . . How are you?"

"We're all fine too . . . Is Pat there?"

"What do you want to say to her?"

"I just felt like talking to her."

"She's out."

"Oh . . . Well, actually I called because I was wondering if she might . . . come down again."

"We don't have the money for that, Kate."

"I can pay for it, Mom . . ."

"Pat's too young to travel alone."

"She came before."

"I know."

"Why don't you come too? It's not that expensive if you come by bus. Jill is so great now. She talks so well . . . I should think being her grandmother, you'd want to see how she was coming along and all . . ."

"Kate, have you called up just to criticize me for my behavior?"

"No."

"How is Sam?"

"Okay, he's not here right this second."

"Oh?"

"He's . . . rehearsing."

"Where?"

"I don't know . . . He moved out."

"Are you getting another divorce, then?"

"No, it's not . . . He just. It's hard for him with my knee . . . He just—and he doesn't have a job yet."

"You mean he still doesn't have a job! I can't *believe* that!"

"Mom, stop it, will you!"

"That to me is simply scandalous."

"Okay . . . Listen, if Pat comes in later, tell her what I said, okay? That she should come down."

"I don't know, Kate . . . Pat is so young. I don't want her getting into all kinds of trouble."

"What kind of trouble is she going to get into playing with Jill and helping me clean up the apartment?"

"You know what I mean."

"I *don't* know what you mean."

"I should think now that you're a mother, you would understand. Mothers worry—"

"Okay, okay . . . Forget it, then. It was great talking to you, Mom. I'd forgotten what a sweetheart you are. So long."

I'm shivering. I'm turning to ice. Ugh. Why did I do that? Why did I call? Why in the name of anything did I tell her Sam had left? It's weird how you do certain things again and again, get the same reaction and yet go on expecting a different one. She doesn't have to know Sam has left. So why did I tell her? To make her feel sorry for me maybe, all alone? To make her send Pat down? . . . But that never works with her. She hates people who beg for things from her. She thinks pride is the most important virtue in the world . . . Why did I tell her Sam doesn't have a job? I guess, indefensible as it is, I want to be honest with her. If I lied and pretended things that weren't so, it would seem to be proving all she said of me was true. It isn't that I knew Pat would come down and see Sam wasn't here and go back and tell her. I just want there to be truth and openness between us. Bullshit, as Sam would say. You have to build openness on something and we don't have that something.

I fall asleep late, really late. For awhile I lie awake listening to the tapes I've done. It's funny hearing your own voice. I don't quite sound like me. But that must be how I sound to others ... I don't listen long. Talking to Mom got me too down, way down. I want to sleep.

All of a sudden, I hear footsteps. My heart starts pounding. Don't let it be a burglar. We have nothing to rob. I call out loudly, "Who is it?" hoping that if they know someone's home, they'll go away.

"Bob Dylan," A voice says. It's Sam!

He comes into the room, guitar on his back, carrying a funny-looking tiger cat. Seeing the tape recorder, he grins. "Making love to your machine?"

"It's a nice alternative," I say, staring him down. "It doesn't walk out when things get sticky. It doesn't argue. It's not stupid. Or bullheaded—"

"Well, I hope the two of you have a wonderful life together." He hands me the cat. "This character was hanging around *O'Brien's* . . . I thought you might like him." He walks past me into the bedroom.

I begin stroking the cat. What a funny creature, one ear looks like it's mashed down on one side. "Did you come back for your stuff?"

"Yeah."

"Odd time to move, isn't it?"

"Jill's asleep."

"So it's easier?"

"Much easier."

I watch him as he begins taking things out of the drawer and throwing them in his bag. "Want me to shut up too? Or doesn't it matter one way or the other?"

"I'm immune to you."

I just stand there, watching him. It's as though he was at the wrong end of a telescope, a million miles away, very small. A strange feeling. "What's the cat's name?"

"Gypsy."

"Is that symbolic or something?"

"Descriptive."

"I like him . . . He seems to like me."

"He's dumb. He might."

I can't help smiling, he's trying so hard not to say one nice thing. "I miss you and your snotty remarks."

Sam turns. After a second he says, "I miss you too . . . You and your death wish."

"That's gone."

"Sure."

"I mean it."

He looks puzzled. "You're going to take the drugs?"

I shake my head. Then suddenly I find myself saying, "Let's go to the mountains, Sam, away from all this, you and me and Jill. It would be so good . . ."

"It would be the same."

"It wouldn't have to be."

"What about the cancer? What're you going to do about it?"

"Live with it."

"You're asking me to watch you die, baby . . . I can't."

"I'm not . . . Don't watch me die . . . Just stay for now . . . Please, Sam. I beg you . . . If you can't take it at the end, then go."

Slowly, he puts down his guitar and comes over to me. I'm not going to cry. I just stand there and let him hold me. "People do things different ways," I say, very low. "Just respect my way, that's all. Understand it."

He strokes my hair. "I missed you a lot . . . I wanted you a lot."

"I wanted you . . . It's been lousy. I called Mom tonight."

He laughs. "You must have been desperate!"

"I wanted Pat to come down. She said no."

"That figures."

"How's it going, with your rehearsing and all?"

We lie on the bed together. "It's good." But he isn't paying attention. He's moving toward me, on top of me, his lips on mine.

Okay, so I had no pride, Mom, and it worked. So you're wrong, see? Sometimes it works. I don't have time for pride.

Autumn is the time for loneliness
and love
That died in the forgotten sun.

The time for being alone
in your world
to decide answers for all the questions
that summer brought.

The time to write unfinished poems
and sing unfinished songs
before winter freezes them forever.

The time to end,
and begin again
as we always do,
anyway . . .

Finally. Peace, within myself. Summer is over and fall is my time, my poetry. I love it. September and changing leaves, falling, cluttering, drifting to the ground. The smell of the sun, the dying grass, the light filtering through the branches. In autumn the sun is in the peace position. It's time for warm sweaters and football and touching and loving. Oh, I love it all so much.

It's been good since Sam came back. Of course, he's not always around, but I wouldn't want that. He has to have his music. I would never ask him to give that up just to be with me. Anyway, I have my tapes and that makes a lot of difference. Sometimes, I think I'm trying too hard to say something meaningful in them. Sometimes, my mind just goes blank. I don't feel at ease. It's hard to put it down when I'm worried Sam will hear it all eventually. It's not that I have anything to say that he shouldn't read, but it's hard to write about things that hurt and things that need to be thought out privately when you know someone else will be reading them.

Still, I feel like I've come to terms with things more, whether because of the tapes or Sam being understanding or what. Cancer is really a very bad disease, that's true, but I think there're other things I wouldn't want to have either. I don't think I would want to have Multiple Sclerosis or, I don't know, something that would make me lose my mind somehow but still let me retain my body. I wouldn't want to be mentally retarded. I wouldn't want to have to be normal in every respect and yet not able to communicate with people. I didn't think it would be as easy to cope with just having cancer. I mean, cancer hurts. You get it and it grows and it grows and you know that your chances are very slim. It seems like, though, there are other things that are at least just as bad. What I'm trying to say is that I'm not that badly off, even though I'm dying. There're worse ways to go, I guess. I don't know, maybe I won't feel that way at the end if it hurts much worse and I can't breathe. Even now I get tired fast, I can't do so much around the house. So I don't know how I'll feel later when it gets worse than this. Maybe I won't feel that way at all.

The dilemmas of dying are many. You can't figure out if you want to be buried or cremated, embalmed or not, what clothes you want to be buried in, what you want on your gravestone. What is natural? That's what I have to decide. Or at least what would feel most natural to me. What would give me the best chance of getting back to this earth if reincarnation does happen? I mean, you read ashes to ashes, dust to dust . . . What does that mean?

I guess I like the idea of cremation for the thought of having my ashes spread across the mountains. I see Sam, standing tall, the wind whipping his long hair, with a beautiful vase in his hand, tossing my ashes out into the wind, quickly dissipating into nothingness, gone as quickly as I came into the world so many years ago.

That's so romantic, though, and that is the only part of cremation I can think of that I like. I envision myself being burned, the flesh snapping and crackling in the fire, my flesh falling away from the bone. No, maybe I don't want to be cremated.

So that leaves being buried. I hate the thought of being stuffed inside a box and put into the ground. I dig the idea of having a gravestone to write something on, though. I like the idea of having some music played for me and would like the idea of flowers if they weren't from the florist, I mean, so deathly-looking. They should be beautiful, free-form, field flowers— Queen Anne's lace, roses, daisies, to signify not just death, but a passing on, a freedom that I will have achieved.

I want just to be buried in a pair of shorts or one of the skirts Sam bought me, and a comfortable shirt, not something stiff and unnatural. I want just a simple wood coffin, with old-fashioned handles and a soft plush inside and a nice pillow. I don't want a metal casket, that isn't natural. How can you return to the earth in a metal that won't rot?

The music I want is John Denver's *Country Roads*.

Today I tried to write a poem for Jill, but all I could think of—the only word beautiful enough—was

Beautiful Sunshine

That's what she is to me and no other words express it. So, no poem, Jill—but much love, much care, much giving to you.

When we're up in the mountains, it's almost as if I can forget everything bad, the bitter thoughts and think only constructively. Then we come back and real life is there; going to the hospital, all of that.

This time when we pull up in front of our apartment, Weaver is sitting on our steps. "Where've you been?" he says to Sam. "We had an audition. We had a job. Nearly. Except you weren't there."

I glance at Sam. I didn't know he'd had an audition. If I'd known, I'd never have suggested we get away this weekend. It was my birthday, that was why I wanted to go this particular weekend—I'm twenty now, not a teen-ager anymore. A grown up lady, a woman. Still, even my birthday could've waited. If what Weaver says is true. You never can tell with him.

We all go inside and Sam brings the groceries we got on the way back into the kitchen. "We had to go to the mountains," he says.

"Without telling anybody?" Weaver says. "I mean,

you knew about the audition, man . . . What're you doing?"

"Lay off," Sam says.

I guess he doesn't want to say it was my birthday. Not that Weaver would consider that a very good excuse. I go in to get a fresh Pamper for Jill. As I'm passing Weaver, he says, "How's the big C, Kate?"

He hates me so much! Wow, I suppose I should feel honored. But it just makes me feel rotten. I knew coming home would be a matter of coming down to earth, but I thought it would be drifting down gradually, not falling with a thud on pointed rocks. I don't even answer, just go to Jill.

Sam says angrily, "I said, lay off."

"I was feeling a lot better before you showed up, thanks," I can't help putting in.

"Oh, right," Weaver says. "Now you're going to have to rush right back up to the mountains, aren't you, to recuperate from nasty old Weaver . . . Your old man doesn't need to work."

"Weaver," Sam says.

But he goes on in that same sarcastic voice. "Nothing is more important than dying. You don't need money, you're 'above' money. You don't have hospital bills. Rent. Gas. You don't buy shoes. Jill never needs shoes . . . It's really a great life. As long as you've got parents you can soak."

Sam grabs him. For a second I think he's going to sock him one and almost wish he would. But he just turns away. He looks depressed.

Weaver goes on, "The guys they got, it's pathetic. Keith Wilder and Gordon Matthews. Sam, you *know* we're better than they are. You know we would've gotten the job if only we'd been there. If only she—"

"It's my fault," Sam says. "Leave Kate out of this."

I look at him, but he's looking at Weaver who's set-tled into a chair. Weasel would be a better name for him with those little eyes and scruffy hair. "I'm split-ting," he says.

"Good," I say.

"The group?" Sam is shaken, I can tell.

"I've got to make money."

"Sam'll do better as a single," I say.

"He won't do anything as a single."

"Sam, are you hungry? Do you want a beer?"

"Sure, thanks."

"I'll have one too," Weaver says.

I get two beers and hand one to each of them. "What do you need money for?" I say. "You eat all our food. You drink all our beer."

"Well, you've wrecked my life," he says. "I might as well be into you for something."

"Oh come on. Wrecked your life! How?"

"I came all the way up here, knowing Sam and I could form a good group . . . I could've stayed in Den-ver and—"

"Oh bull! You did what you wanted, Weaver! Don't dump it on us!"

"Why do you think I won't make it as a single?" Sam says carefully.

How can Sam take him seriously? I get so angry at that. "He's jealous, that's why. He knows he won't make it as a single because he's such a nurd and he's scared you will."

"I love you too, baby." He looks at Sam. "Okay, I'll tell you why, since we're having a big truth session here . . . You don't work any more, even *when* you work, if you follow me. Your head's not there . . . And—you just don't work enough. Christ, remember when we were starting, we used to work every night, night after night . . . Music doesn't mean enough to you anymore."

There's a long silence.

"That's a dumb lie," I say.

"No, it's the truth," Sam says quietly. "What'll you do, on your own?" he says to Weaver, not angry.

"I used to sell stuff," Weaver says. "Before I ran into you and Givits." He looks over at me. "Hey, Kate, you're at the hospital a lot. You've got access. How about it? . . . Seems like you kind of owe it to me, kid."

I look at Sam, startled.

"That's not very funny," he says.

"It wasn't meant to be."

"Then get out."

"Who? Me—or her?"

"Get out before I kill you."

"Oh, wow . . ." He raises his beer can. "I want to drink to this early John Wayne on my left."

Sam gets up and grabs the can out of Weaver's hand and hurls it across the room. It hits the wall and beer dribbles down on the floor. Weaver gets up. In a mocking voice he says, "And don't come back till you've apologized to my wife."

"Right."

"Forget it, pal, forget it." He walks out, slamming the door.

I stare after him. "Thank God . . . I wish he'd left months ago . . . I wish he'd never come here after you."

"He's a damn fine musician," Sam says slowly.

"So what! I don't care *what* he is! He's a rotten, mean person."

Sam rubs my shoulders. "I'm sorry, Kate."

"If he's such a damn fine musician, why's he so scared stiff about making it without you?"

"Well, together, we were good . . . Look, I think he's right, frankly. I'll never make it by myself, either."

"So, you'll form some other group."

"Sure, only—"

"Anyway, how do you know? Maybe you *could* make it alone. Just because *he* says—"

"No, I couldn't, Kate . . . I don't mean I'm not good. I'm not knocking myself . . . Look, we had something good, the three of us. He was right. We would've gotten the job. I just feel it."

"Then blame him . . . for walking out now. Don't blame me!"

After a second he says, "I'm not blaming you."

"It was my birthday. That's why we went . . . Why didn't you tell him that?"

He shrugs.

"We didn't even have to go . . . Why didn't you tell me you had the audition? I would've understood."

He just looks pained. "I guess I should've. I just thought—"

"What?"

"I don't know."

"Sam, listen, we've got to be honest with each other. Without that, it's just stupid, it doesn't make any sense."

"Yeah, you're right." He sits down. "I don't know . . ."

"What?"

"I just think maybe he's right . . . My heart isn't in it anymore. You have to give all of yourself to it."

"Well, then give it, if that's what you want! Don't sit around waiting for me to die so you can do that! That's sick! How does that make me feel?"

"I can't, Kate . . . I don't have it in me."

"Okay, then accept that."

"I try to . . . Then I think, if only this hadn't happened."

"My getting sick?"

He nods, not looking at me.

"I know!"

"I guess I don't believe in God especially," he says, "but if he does exist, he ought to be drawn and quartered . . . He must be some sick joke artist."

"Maybe he's like Weaver," I say, smiling. "I mean, he just happened to have this knack for stuff like creating the world and man and all . . . But he's a moral idiot, he has a pea for a brain when it comes to anything else."

Sam smiles. We sit side by side. I rub his hand. "You're good," I say.

"Am I?"

"Yes." I can't say anything more, though I'd like to.

"Where's Jill?"

"Inside . . . sleeping."

He glances up. "How long do you think she'll—" He draws me down on the bed.

"Long enough."

The sun is streaming in the window. Beautiful sunshine.

How's this for anti-climaxes? Weaver and Sam are back together again. It was Givits who "reconciled" them which I think was sweet in a way. He said they had so much going together, it was a shame to break it up now, that they should just put personal differences to one side. There's kind of a prickly, competitive thing between Weaver and Sam, whereas Givits always seems older. They both listen to him. I'm not sure he really is that much older—it's his manner. Anyway, be that as it may, they're off rehearsing again, auditioning.

I'm glad. I don't want the guilt of feeling Sam wrecked his career for my sake. Like all those crummy movies on the late late show. He ruined his career for a mere woman. Not that the mere woman part appeals to me, but music and Sam are too much one to be parted. And maybe he's right. He may be good, but not in a way that would show to best advantage in solo.

It makes me laugh, though. After that big "scene". I guess life is like that. Pulling these little surprises.

Today Sam is off rehearsing and I'm lying here, day-dreaming. I like to sometimes, to go into the past. Guess there's not too much future to think about. I remember that first day Sam and I spent together, not the one we met, but the day after, after I'd spent the night at his place. We had coffee and toast and kept staring at each other. Doing all those things together, brushing our teeth etc. seemed so natural. He had this big black hat on, probably stolen from some theatre set, which really made him look dramatic. He showed me some pictures he'd painted, water color sketches. I liked them. I liked his apartment which was small, but looked comfortable, lived in. It gave me a feeling of being home. He played the guitar for me like a mad-man, shouting with joy the few songs he knew, some-times drawing his brows together as if that would make him sound better. Then gently, he would stroke the strings to make the music he had written in his head, bending over the guitar like it was a precious gift. He played with such compassion and finesse. He's a great guitarist because he loves what he does and plays from his heart. Sometimes, he plays when he's sad and it's so beautiful I want to cry, but don't because he's so sensi-tive and tender that he would never play again that way if I did.

I like his eyes. They can look so fierce and wicked with passionate hate for what he dislikes and sometimes so round and innocent and so deep I can see far into them. They hold a lot of love for almost everything he touches. I like what we have between us now. It's been scratchy lately, but it's growing back. We love together, just him and me and our little Jill and no one gets in unless we want them. We need only each other. I love Sam because he's warm and compassionate, because he says to me, "Kate, I love you" and I know he means it.

I don't ever want to leave him. I love him. Now I'm thinking how unfair it is. A tear wells up and creeps down my cheek. Love is not something you can live or die without.

I wonder why I haven't heard from the hospital. Last week they took a new series of tests to see how things were going. I would've expected they would call to tell me the results. I'm worried. I'm afraid I know already. I guess it makes no difference.

I had some pretty strong thoughts on dying last night. When I'm lying in bed, it's so hard not to think about it. It's so damned unfair. To me, to Jill, to Sam. I just can't understand it at all. I can't understand the way all of this works into the scheme of things. Why doesn't it at least have some purpose! It has only brought me pain and my family pain. Why?

Sam is right, though. I've still got a lot of living to do before it's time to die. Guess I should do some. My time is running short. I should make a list of all the things I want to do before I die. There are so many things!

I want to finish my book for Jill. I want a piano. I want to learn to play beautiful songs. I always have wanted to, but somehow never got around to it. I want to finish the quilt I started and some tea towels and pillow cases and sheets to put in a cedar chest for Jill and I want to put some other things in too. I don't know what exactly. Just little things she'll need someday. Mostly a lot of love.

I want to make things good between Sam and me. I know the best thing I could do would be to make love the way we used to, but I just can't, it hurts so. I want to give him so much, whatever there is I can do to prove my love and devotion. I wish I could give him of all things a motorcycle. But more than commercial

things, material things, I want to give him all of myself.
If I'm any good at all, then he truly deserves me, for he
deserves any and all things that are good.

There are lots of little things I want to do. Fill this
book, knit Sam a sweater. Grow my hair long. I pray
for time.

Going to the hospital. That familiar building. I don't dread it any more. They've been good to me and that means a lot. At first, when I went to Riverdale and found out that I had cancer, I felt only fear and anger and worst of all hate toward the medical profession for not having something to help me with. But after coming to Niles, I feel so very different. I've learned so much that I'm actually, in ways, thankful for the opportunities I've had, from being sick. They've all been so kind and thoughtful that I can't help but think of the hospital as an island in my high sea of trouble. When I come there, I feel very safe and cared for and that's quite a change from the fear I used to know.

I'm so glad they understood, finally, about my going off the drugs. I think they saw that for some people it really is better to die in peace of mind than in the turmoil that I felt about the situation. If a person can accept the drugs and the pain of it all, then I say, right

on, give the best you've got. But to those who can't,
I'm glad they had the insight to let it be. I love them,
and especially Dr. Gillman, a lot for that. It really has,
I feel, given me a lot of inner strength.

"Sam will meet me here later," I tell Dr. Gillman.
"He said the audition would be over at nine-forty,
but—"

She's looking at me in a funny way. "Has he got the
adoption papers for Jill yet?"

"No, he hasn't even applied . . . Why?"

"Here it is, Kate."

Somehow, I knew today would be the day. I knew it
when I woke up, but, still, at her words, something
freezes inside me and my mouth gets dry. We look at
the x-ray together. The spot is there. It's in the lung.

"How much time does that leave me?"

"Not much."

"Weeks? Months? Days?"

"It's hard to say."

When Sam comes to pick me up, he looks so elated,
I don't say anything. He's sure they did well this time,
that they may have a job. "Keep your fingers crossed,
baby."

"I will."

I feel badly that just as things are working for him,
I'm going. Not just for me, but I wish I could be more
a part of his happiness.

When we come home, he tucks me into bed and
turns on the t.v., then goes out. Where? To Nora? I
have the feeling he's slept with her, maybe in that time
we were apart. Just from little things he's let drop. No,
I haven't found lipsticked handkerchiefs in his pocket.
Well, she knew things were bad with us, I told her . . .
and he needs someone, someone alive, living. I understand it. Still, I have moments of feeling bitter like now

when he just vanishes and leaves me here alone. I think I've become repulsive sitting in bed. I'm getting upset by the whole situation. If I am repulsive, if I am upsetting to be with, boring to be with, then please, God, do something so that our relationship isn't wrecked, so that there's something good to remember at the end. For surely neither of us need the pain that not getting along brings us.

Sam doesn't realize what it's like, I don't think. When I get to feeling down, he thinks I'm just feeling sorry for myself. I know I do, but is that so wrong? I'm losing an awful lot and it's not really easy. But he could help by being kinder sometimes. I don't know. Maybe it's just me. Lately he seems different, maybe because his music is going better and he's so involved in that again. It seems like he's always acting up in front of friends, trying to make them notice him, doing things he would never have done before. He doesn't care about his appearance anymore. I used to love it so much when he dressed nice. And he did too, but now, sometimes I'm ashamed of how he looks. Maybe that's petty, but it's important to me that he looks nice. It shows that he cares. Maybe he just doesn't care anymore. I wish he'd wait to be a slob till I die. I love him for the way he is inside. Not all the stuff he's been doing to impress people. It confuses me. I don't know. I guess I love him despite myself.

Jill has been gone this weekend visiting Sam's parents. I miss the little stinker so much. She's been my rod, my staff through my whole sickness. She's been my comfort and I desperately need her. I shouldn't have sent her away. Still, it's been good for Sam. I guess I'm bitter. I get bitter when I can't go to the bathroom and Sam has to bring me the bed pan. Or when my leg drips gory, ugly juices. I feel so repulsive. I feel bitter when I look at pictures of Jill and realize that soon I won't even be able to see pictures of her. I won't get to touch her or be with her or remember her. Oh, how I wish that at least in death you could remember. I wonder if you can. I doubt it. Death being not proud. What does that mean, I wonder. It means to me that death isn't afraid to come and take you away, no matter who you are, which is upsetting. I have so much to give, so many things to do, so many people to be—and I'm not going to get to do it.

Sam has a job! He came back late last night so excited. I am too. It's at *O'Brien's*, that place they used to hang out. They have a great audience, he said, people that know music, people that buy records. Maybe in six months they'll have an album out. He was so pleased, so happy, that I got carried along and that was good. Since I'd heard that news at the hospital, I'd been really low. Now my mood seems to have lifted. Jill is back, talking away, chattering about everything, seeming so happy. Just seeing the two of them like that, into their own things, makes me feel good. The job is two nights a week. I'm so proud of Sam. He's wanted this for so long.

When something good like this happens, you kind of regret a lot of other things. I regret that ugly scene with Weaver that time. Even though I think he was mean. Now, since they got the job, he's actually been nice to me. Trying to be, anyway.

191

Givits may get married. He was here with his girl, her name is Maria. I liked her. She thinks he's the greatest thing that ever lived.

"He married us," I say. I'm tucked up in my blanket, feeling warm and snug. I like to remember that day.

"How was it?" she asks. "Was he good?"

"It was wonderful . . . sort of crazy, though. It was in the hospital."

"Oh?" She looks uneasy. Does she know about me? Maybe just that I'm sick.

"We'd just come here, we weren't even planning on it, we just thought we'd live together like we had been, but then—my divorce papers came through and—"

Givits and Sam are talking about something with their music.

"Your little girl is so sweet," Maria says. "She gave me this." She shows me a small doll.

"Yeah, she likes to do that, to give people presents."

"Aren't you excited—about their opening night?"

"Oh sure . . . It'll be great . . . I probably won't go, though. I'm not sure I—"

"Of course you'll go!" Sam says loudly. "What do you mean?"

I don't feel like talking about it in front of them so I just say, "I guess I will then."

When they go, Sam goes in to give Jill her bath. I'm just not up to that anymore. It tires me too much. Anyhow, I think she really digs having him fix it for her, towel her off. I don't blame her. I used to be like that with my Dad.

I tried writing my parents a letter a few nights ago, but I don't know. Is it worth it? I guess I wanted to try to say all I felt, especially about how it's been bad these last few years. But it didn't come out right. More sort of pleading which I didn't want. But suddenly the phone rings and it's Mom. I can tell from her voice she feels she had to call. There's that "duty" sound, not especially a loving sound.

"I gather Sam is back?" she says. "You said—"

"Yeah, he ... He's even got a job!"

"What type of job does he have?"

"Playing the guitar ... That's what he does, you know." Oh, don't let me get mad at her. Why does she have to sound that way, like an FBI agent?

"Does he get paid?"

"Of course he gets paid, Mom ... He belongs to the union. They have to pay him ... It's a regular job."

In the background I can hear Jill splashing around and Sam playing with her.

"How much does he get paid?"

"A lot! ... Mom, listen—"

Luckily, just as I'm about to blow my cool, once and for all, Sam comes in and takes the phone from me. "Hi, Mother? This is King Kong and I'll tell you how much I get paid. I get paid four thousand dollars a week, and we're going to buy this fantastic mansion with six swimming pools and a gold bathroom and maybe, maybe if you're real good, you can come visit us. Okay?" And he hangs up.

I'm laughing, out of nervousness mainly, but I can't stop. I double over, clutching my sides.

"Your mother is a real mother, you know that?" he says, going back to Jill.

"You shouldn't have, Sam."

"Shouldn't have! ... I should've said a lot more that I'm just too polite and well-bred to say to a lady."

"Why is she like that, though?"

"Honey, you know the answer to that."

"But, like, her life was hard, but was it so much harder than anyone else's?" I begin thinking of Sam's mother of whom I've certainly voiced various ill-humored comments in my time. Only—she loves Sam. I mean, say whatever you like about her, she's narrow-minded or petty or has the wrong values, but she loves him, right down to her toes, even when she can't understand why he does what he does—and she rarely can. Still, there's always that rock-bottom thing which is there, no matter what.

Jill comes shrieking out of the tub. "Put your nightgown on, baby!" Sam says, running after her.

"I don't want to!" Jill says, leaping up on the bed with me. "I want to tuck in with Mommy."

"Hon, you'll be cold with nothing on." But she is already deep down under the covers, the sheet pulled up to her chin, looking at us with mischievous eyes. I peek under the sheet. "I see a belly button down there."

She squirms up and pulls up my shirt. "I see Mommy's belly button." She pushes against my breasts, what there is of them now that I'm so thin. Playfully she squeezes them. "Some day Jill will have breasts too," I say.

She looks thoughtful, considering this. "I don't want them . . . They flop!"

"Not necessarily."

"I'm not going to have them," she declares.

"Okay, hon."

"Hey, ladies," Sam calls from the kitchen. "Are you two going to rise for supper . . . Or shall I serve you in bed?"

"In bed!" Jill yells, excited.

"No, we'll get up," I say. I hate being that much of an invalid. I can still make it to the table, at least.

"Shall I heat up this chicken?"

"Sure." I hate it that Sam has do everything now, all the cooking, tidying up. He's good about it, he doesn't complain, but I don't like it. That's old fashioned, I guess. But I did like cooking and keeping the house nice. I miss doing those things.

❧

Boy, Sam's mother doesn't let anything go by, does she? She had to go and get Mr. George to get the adoption papers for Jill. Christ, I hate to think what Sam would do without her. Jesus, if she doesn't lay off, Sam is never going to do anything for himself. I realize she is maybe trying to be helpful, but she is just one big nuisance. She's so sure she's going to get Jill. I'll bet— well. I won't say, but I bet my wishes won't be carried out when I die. She finally told Sam's father about everything and tried to blame the fact that we hadn't told him before on me. I remember asking both her and Sam to tell him—but no, it had to be their way. I don't know what they planned to do when Jill got old enough to know the truth.

Sam can sense I'm irritated about it. "Look, hon, I just haven't had time. With our show opening in a day or so."

"I know!"

"I'll take care of Jill. The papers are in my name."

"You'll be too busy. With your work and all—"

"I'll find a way."

I want to believe him so much I let myself believe him. What happens will happen. What I say doesn't matter much, I guess. And really if Jill is happy that is the main thing. Ideally, I would like her raised by someone who felt as I do about life. I'm sure there are such people in the world, I'm not a freak, but none where it's a viable alternative. So the next best is that she be raised in a way that brings her happiness. After all, I don't exactly approve of how my parents raised me, but I still had a lot of happiness as a child and have certainly had a lot as an adult. It's just stupid to aggravate myself with torments over Jill's future. Children are strong. And somehow I feel she will remember me, even if not in any conscious way. What we've had together will be there and she can come back to that.

This dying thing is getting to be such a drag. I've been sitting in bed all day long because my chest hurts too much to move. Just now I got up to go to the bathroom for the first time and my leg started bleeding extremely hard and fast. It scared me so much. I don't know what to do, it's all so scary.

The raindrops are falling down my window like molten jewels. The car lights flicker and sparkle as the tires write melodies splashing the water against the curbs.

My chest is hurting so very badly. I spend my days now, sitting up in Sam's lounge chair or in bed, propped by pillows, trying hard, struggling sometimes, to breathe. The t.v. is my constant companion. I watch all the repeats, the specials, the soap operas, laughing at the last, because my life would fit so well in that market.

I haven't written any poems lately, haven't felt like it. I've had so many thoughts to categorize, so many fears and ideas, so angry with myself for being sick. Here's one from a few weeks ago that I worked over a little:

I can't see you
in another's arms—
smoothing back the wrinkles
on your forehead.

I can't help but cry
to think of another
telling you it's okay
when you've had a lonely day

Seems like only yesterday
I began to share your bed
and like the gentle rain,
you've let share your head.

I hate to see it end
and yet baby
maybe things will be better
when the days are shorter
with the winter of my life—
and finally freedom in the spring.

I've been thinking lately
of my life
It's been a good one,
nice just to hang around.
how long it's been since this mornin'
Seems like it was only yesterday, my baby.

I play with Gypsy, my cat. Ah, she's so wicked. Grabbing me with feet and mouth, so feisty. Never does she use her claws or teeth, she's so loyal. She sleeps with me at night, lies with me all day, leaving only to eat or go outside for awhile. I think she thinks I'm her mother.

Sam comes in, gives me a kiss. Kind of a perfunctory one, but maybe I'm getting hyper-sensitive. "That's not the usual kiss," I say, half to myself.

He grins. "I'm higher than a kite, that's all . . . In exactly six hours we hit the big time."

"I know . . . I wish I could be there."

"You're going to be there."

"Jill's just got over her cold. I don't—"

"You're going to leave her . . . Nora said she'll take her . . . I want you with me."

I look at him, puzzled. There's something a little funny, not quite direct here. Should I push it? "What's going on, Sam?"

He looks pained, trapped. "I just want you there. What's wrong with that?"

I can't answer. I don't know the answer.

"Kate? What's wrong with that? Tell me."

Finally, I look right at him. I can't bear this game-playing between us. It makes me sad. "Are you having an affair?"

"You can't stand anybody else in center stage, can you?"

"That wasn't the question."

"Daddy!" Jill calls from the kitchen.

"The answer obviously is no." Sam says, still uncomfortable, not quite looking at me. "Absolutely and categorically no."

"Say that without squirming."

"Daddy!"

He goes in to Jill, glad to escape. I didn't want to make you feel guilty, Sam. It doesn't matter. Is there a way to say that that sounds believable, not phony? I call after him, "Sam . . . it's okay."

I sigh. If I'm going tonight, I'd better take a pain pill just before I set out. Sitting that long, all that noise—I better not pass out, that would be great. I do want to go, but in some ways I feel it might spoil it for Sam, seeing me looking so awful and gaunt.

We leave Jill with Nora. Jill is sleepy and goes without a protest. I'm glad. I don't have the strength to argue with her tonight. We drive to *O'Brien's* and go in the back entrance. Weaver and Givits are already there, nervously fiddling around, tuning up.

"Well, hallelujah!" Weaver says as we appear.

"It's about time!" Givits says.

"We're late," Weaver says. "We were supposed to go on five minutes ago."

"Cool it guys, okay?" Sam says. He sets down his guitar and propels me out into the main room.

The room seems to come up and smash me in the face—the noise, the colors, the smoke. I haven't been out among people, except to go to the hospital, in so long. I feel dizzy, but sort of excited. People are so beautiful! It's like I'd never seen people before. The way they're dressed, in their bright, crazy clothes. I feel so apart from them, like an old lady in my shawl. Sam settles me at a small table up close. In some ways I'd rather be way back, out of sight, but he wants me where he can see me. Okay.

"If you want another beer, tell them," he says. He's very nervous, I can tell.

I don't feel nervous. I know they'll be good. That's not exactly an objective judgment, I realize, but I know that once they get up there, their nervousness will go away. Still, the few moments before they get started, I watch them a little anxiously. There's so much noise. Everyone around me is talking, laughing, as though the three of them were invisible. They struggle around, getting their equipment plugged in.

"Ladies and gentlemen!" Sam yells over the voices. "Hippies, winos, whoever you are out there, may I have your attention, *por favor?* . . . Hey!"

Finally the place quiets down and they begin. It's beautiful. Sam looks at me, then away. I feel glad I came. There's pain, but the pill has removed me a little from it, as though it were some external thing. At one point, I start to cough a little from the smoke and have a minute of panic about my breathing, but it passes. Go slow, Kate. The music weaves in and out of the smoke, the pain, the people's faces, like one giant, beautiful tapestry. Sam is singing *My Sweet Lady*. He's singing to me. I feel stoned, dazzled, floating around and above the whole thing. Oh Sam. I love you.

"Tired?" Sam says. It's real late, maybe two or so. He's in high spirits. It went so well. I feel zapped, like I'd been on a roller coaster that suddenly took a deep, deep dip down and I was hanging onto the sides, hoping I wouldn't fall off.

"Wasn't it incredible?" I say. "I thought they were never going to listen ... Then I thought they were never going to clap."

"It was great." He carries me up the walk. I put my arms around his neck. I guess I don't weigh too much now.

Sam deposits me gently on the bed. I lie back, exhausted.

"Want me to get Jill or shall we leave her down there for the night?"

In the past we would have left her because it would have meant more privacy, the chance of making love in the morning if we felt like it. "What time is it?"

"Two thirty."

"Let's get her in the morning," I say. It seems so quiet here after all that dazzling noise, it's almost unreal.

"How did you feel?" Sam says. "Were you okay?"

I nod. "Once there was a lot of smoke and I . . . But then it was okay."

He's rummaging around in the kitchen. "Want something? Some milk?"

Sam used to make me great milk drinks when I was having cramps from my period, warm milk with a cinnamon stick and sugar. I don't feel too hungry, but I say, "Sure . . . That would be nice."

While he's heating it up, I lie back, just looking around the room. "Sam, did you move the tape recorder?"

"What?" he calls in.

"Did you put it away or something? . . . It's not here. I always keep it right next to the bed."

He comes in. "I didn't touch it." Suddenly he turns around. "The door. I always lock the door. It was open when we came back."

"Oh Jesus!"

"What else did they take, I wonder." He begins looking around. The t.v. is gone too and the radio.

"Remember, Mrs. Whatshername said someone broke into her place a couple of weeks ago."

"Sam, the tape recorder! What'll I do?"

"It wasn't your fault . . . Dr. Gillman won't mind."

"No, but I . . . hadn't finished . . . There's still more I have to do . . . Did they take the tapes? Go check. They're in the drawer over there."

"They're still there."

"Thank God they didn't take them too."

He shakes his head. "I guess it was quite a haul for a small apartment."

"What do you think they wanted with a tape record-er?"

"They could sell it, I guess." He sits down next to me. "Kate, I'm sorry ... Maybe Dr. Gillman can get you another or borrow another—"

"I feel she trusted me with it ... If I hadn't gone—"

"Thank God you did! Imagine if you'd been here alone with Jill!"

"Yeah, that's right, I guess."

"We'll call her tomorrow first thing ... I'm sure she can lend you another."

"I guess it doesn't matter much ... I always feel like there's still so much left to say. But maybe that's always the way you feel." I sip the milk which is warm and comforting.

"Will you get a motorcycle now?" I ask, "now that we're rich?"

He grins. "Yeah, I'd like to, kind of."

"You'll be careful, though, won't you, I mean, not going too fast?"

"Sure."

I sigh and lean back.

"Do you want another pill?" Sam asks.

"Maybe I better."

We lie down together. He holds me and strokes me, what there is left of me. There's nothing to say.

Sam falls asleep and I lie awake. My chest hurts, despite the pills. I lie, watching the lights pass across the room. I feel like it, right now, like death. I get so close at night.

Death can come. Let it touch me now and I won't fight. But I dare it to come when I'm not ready. I have too much to do. My body is drugged with pain pills. I feel so warm and safe. Before I took this past one, I felt hysterical about the robbery. Something is happening to me. Am I getting close to death? I don't know. I feel afraid I am. I feel beautiful, though. Even though I haven't finished my book yet, I know I have at least touched people. Not nearly enough, though. I must work hard. I must give my whole being to Jill, Sam and the book. I'm happy and sad, I'm human and dying, I'm a lot of things, but mostly I'm Kate, wife and lover to Sam, mother and friend to Jill, also . . .

The robbery of the tape recorder has been made into big news in the local paper. Reporters came and interviewed me for t.v. It was grotesque, tiring. They propped me up in bed and asked me questions. Then, at the end they gave me a new tape recorder and a dozen reels of new tape. So I'm a celebrity. Weird. Somehow, the grotesqueness of the whole thing didn't bother me as much as I'd have expected. There's no time for all that, for fineness of feeling, for ultra-sensitivity. I knew in the back of my mind that they were using me, if you want to look at it like that, but so what? It also seemed to me that people genuinely do care, that their sympathy is genuine. Maybe to them I'm like some person they've known that they never grieved for. So now they're all writing me letters, sending things. People from all over the country! A few from other parts of the world even.

What do they send? Oh, anything, everything—Bibles, letters of sympathy, miracle cures, advice. I suppose you can see all the best and worst of people in what they send, the absolute craziness and the sweetness. In the beginning, I was really touched and thought I'd try to answer all the letters. That was when I thought there'd be a dozen or so. Now, after a week, too many are coming in. Nora and Sam just leaf through them, only showing me the "best" ones. Some people send flowers. I'm not gone yet, folks! They mean well, I know.

Lying here, I can hear Nora on the phone. "Hello ... No, this is a friend. Can I help you? ... Well, she can't come to the phone right now, can I take a message?"

Sam forbade me to answer the phone. He's right. Save your strength. I still have my tapes to do and the important thing is to finish. He comes in, shaking his head. "Well, East Germany's got the cure today."

"What is it?"

"Some concoction mixed up in a blender—soybean oil, papaya juice and beet root."

"Ugh."

Nora comes in after him. "Well, get a load of this one," she says, reading. 'God has a reason for everything, Mrs. Hayden, search your soul, find your sin, for you have indeed committed a terrible sin to have brought this terrible punishment on yourself and your loved—' "

Sam snatches it from her and rips it up. "Those people should be boiled in oil."

"Charity, charity!" Nora says mocking.

"I hate those mothers," Sam says. "They're the worst ... The religious crazies ... The health food ones I can take."

I know what he means. They infuriate me too. What

do they mean, have I ever tried Christian Science or being saved by Christ or eating a steady diet of milk and fresh spring water? Do they ever try using their heads? Why do I have this disease in the first place? Why are doctors treating me? If this is truly God's world, then we are truly God's children and are all working to make this a place we can all live in healthfully, happily and peacefully. You don't have to go to church unless you can't do it any other way and you don't have to be saved or even pray formal prayers unless you need that crutch to get you through the day. All you need to do is get your stuff together in your head about how you feel and please don't come to me with Christ in your heart and at the same time supporting the war or spending your time in church instead of being out in the ghetto, helping God's other children in their time of need or instead of teaching little kids Sunday School and Christ loves us, teach them that they must love one another before they can love themselves. Teach them what it is to love and cherish and to respect and to understand. Those are the things that are going to make the world a better place to live in. I don't care how many times you are saved. That doesn't make it okay to sin, just because you figure God will forgive you. Everything you do is closely examined and will reveal itself in the end. Believe me, He's there and if we don't get busy and love one another, then He's not going to love us and we are going to be in a hell of a mess.

End of sermon . . . Well, lying here all day, I tend to go off the deep end at times. But if these people really had love in them, I wouldn't mind their "sermons" to me. But so many of them seem to have these warped, hell and damnation minds. I know what they mean to the extent that I, more than anyone, mind the randomness of this happening, the "no reason" of it. But I prefer that to inventing reasons, especially when those reasons are that all disease is a punishment for sin. Would those people say the same thing if they'd seen those small children at the hospital, dying?

Jill trots over with a Bible and plunks it down on top of the pile. We're getting quite a collection here.

"How about lunch, Kate?"

"Oh, thanks . . . Maybe later."

Nora's been sweet. Sometimes I wish she'd go off and leave us alone, but she's really been helpful, keeping an eye on Jill and stuff. She took her to the playground a couple of times this week so Sam and I could be alone.

I'm so glad Sam has his job, has to practice and keep regular hours. The worst would be to have him sitting around all day, holding my hand, "waiting." I don't even mind when all of them are out and I'm alone. It seems like I've gotten used to being alone, at least part of each day, and I'd miss it. I sit, the blanket around me, and talk into the tape recorder. Gypsy curls up sleepily, kind of half-listening to my voice. Sometimes I play back what I've said on other days. I'm used to the fact that my voice isn't what I think of as my voice. Now, sleepily, I flip it on and listen:

"Jill,

I decided that before I died I wanted to write you a book. I've just begun to realize that that's exactly what I'm doing with this book.

In it I'm trying to write of important things that happened to me, things you'll want to know later. Gee, honey, I wish I could be with you when you're old enough to read this. I wonder what you'll be like. I hope that Dad will be able to teach you all that we had planned together to teach you. By the time you read this, you'll be about fourteen or fifteen years old. I wonder what you'll be like then.

If you ever feel the need of someone to talk to, honey, don't be afraid to come to this book. I know I can't help with all my written words, but please take comfort in knowing that whatever is wrong or whatever has made you hurt, I would have deeply cared and tried my best to understand. Perhaps that will ease the pain somewhat. I love you so much, baby. Take heart in that, please. There are so many things I always wanted to tell my daughter. Perhaps one very important thing I wanted most to say was no matter what, always do what you feel is right or best for you. Not out of selfishness, such as wanting to stay out late when you need rest for a good reason. But out of love for yourself. Treat your body and mind right and they in turn will give you health and beauty.

If you want to sleep with a boy before you're married, please remember that sex is a function humans need to survive, but love is an emotion and through it you can be deeply hurt or given a happiness you will never forget. Don't just sleep with any man for sex. At least feel an affection, a bond of giving and receiving with him. This is so important, Jill, if you are to survive any sort of relationship. And for pete's sake, don't get pregnant. Talk it over with your father. If you know your mind well enough, when and if this time comes, he'll feel it in the way you ask and will understand. Remember, though, he's a sensitive man. Don't hurt him."

Wow! How's that for a lecture and a bit of advice. I hope I don't sound like an old windbag. That's the trouble with this method of communication. I tend to warble on a bit. I don't even talk that way! But I do believe it, and know that it's good and right.

Last night I had a dream that I was on an airplane
and Jill was on it with Sam. She was much older,
maybe a teen-ager, he looked about the same. They
were talking, but I couldn't catch what they were
saying. I kept leaning over, wanting to hear. Then,
toward the end they came over to me. Jill looked so
pretty, long, blond hair to her waist, really grown up,
lovely. She laughed and sort of nudged me and said,
"You haven't done with us yet!" Almost winking like it
was some kind of joke. And then they walked off.

What does it mean, I wonder. I'd like to know what
will happen, what she'll be like. I lie here, thinking of
her at different ages, trying to imagine, her first teacher,
her first boyfriend, and then it mingles in with my own
past and I don't know if I'm remembering or what.

Sam came back after the show tonight. He comes in
quietly, careful not to wake me, but I'm usually awake.
I spend so much of the day in bed, half dozing, that at
night I can't sleep. Also, since the robbery I feel a little
afraid at night, of someone breaking in. I feel relieved
when I hear Sam come in.

"Hi!" I call softly.

"Hi, honey."

"How did it go?"

"Pretty good . . . We tried the new song. I think it
went over."

"Was the audience good?"

"Kind of . . . They can be awfully noisy . . ." He gets
himself a beer. "Want one?"

"Sure."

"Was Jill okay?"

"Yeah, a little lively . . . She wanted me to read to
her so I did."

"Don't let her tire you out."

"I don't . . . I like reading to her."

"How's your chest . . . Is it—"

"The same, more or less."

We talk a little tentatively. What else is there to say? We've said it all, done it all, tried our best. What we had was good and I'm glad I knew that at the time, while it was happening. I could see that looking back you would try to make it out better than it was. But I knew it was good, even the rough spots.

"Want me to play a little for you?"

"Yes." Jill never wakes up when Sam plays, he sings softly. I feel when he sings, he expresses all the things he can't when he speaks. The music goes back and forth between us, like a voice, saying a lot for which there are no words.

I've run out of words. I'm getting so close to death. I look over at Jill and it hurts so bad, knowing that we will soon be losing each other. I don't even know what to say anymore. All my words of sorrow have been spent. I look at Sam. I look at his face. I think of his losing me. And of me losing him. I look at his smooth features. I can see every pore on his skin. I know every scar by heart. His smell, his breathing when he's asleep. I can almost read his mind. I'm going to miss you, honey. The way you touch me and comfort me when I'm sad. The way you love and smile. The way you dance with glee when you're happy. I'm confused, honey, not scared. What's happening to us? Where am I going? I wish in a way that I could say with some conviction that I was going to heaven. It would be so much easier. But being as human as I have become in my lifetime, I don't think I would like heaven. I don't think I would like all that gross perfection.

I can't die and leave you guys! Who's going to yell out to Jill in just the right voice to make her take a nap? Who's going to say to Sam in just the right voice,

"Honey, I love you"? Who's going to clean the toilet or the oven? Who will remember when the cat needs to be wormed? What's the matter with you, God—my family's not a bunch of boy scouts who can figure out all these things for themselves. That's what you taught me to do. That's why I'm here. Why make Sam and Jill grope for answers they'll never understand the questions to? You're some kind of idiot, God, to pull something like this! Especially when you know I don't care if I go to heaven or hell for saying so. What do you gain? I just don't understand.

It's funny to think that in a few more days I probably won't be here. How long can I keep breathing with these rotted lungs? It hurts now, it hurts so bad. I feel fine except for the hurt. I'd like to be up in the mountains. I hope they put me there when I die.

I'm so tired of it all. Tired of the letters and the flowers and the presents. I hope I'm not too bitter. It's hard just to go along and know you're dying. Especially now that it hurts so bad.

It's probably going to be within a week or so. A week or so ... it's so hard to think about it being so soon. So many things I haven't done. What will happen to the book?

When I was expecting Jill, I remember how I packed my suitcase ahead of time to be ready when the time came. If I had my choice, I'd like to die at home, but I know that's not likely. It will be in the hospital. So I have some things in the suitcase, my poems and things. I'm ready.

Will that make it easier, being away from my home, from Jill, from Gypsy? Will it be like one step closer to death? I don't know. If I come back in another life I hope it will be as a cat. I would like to be here, sleeping in the sun, rubbing up against Jill's leg. I think a life as a cat would be fine. Or even as a plant. Growing in the sunlight. That wouldn't be bad, either.

"Kate, do you want your pill?"

It's Sam. I guess I half dozed off while he was playing. Not real sleep, I could hear the music in the background.

I swallow the pill with some beer.

"You'll sleep well now," Sam says, tucking me in.

The last few nights, Jill has woken up with a bad dream. Once I slept right through it and Sam only told me about it in the morning. It's hard to tell if it's a bad dream or what. She'll wake up and come to our bed, wanting comfort. I don't like the idea of being so asleep I don't hear her. I want to be there if she wakes up again.

It's so quiet now.

"Mommy?"

It's Jill, standing near the bed. I reach over to touch her and suddenly something rises up and it's like a bag was thrown over my head. I can't breathe. I can't breathe!

Sam!

PART THREE

In the pastel shades
of winter's easy way
I grasp to feel your hand
to touch, to hear, to see
and understand
why it is life
must be continued
alone
in another land.

I'm in the hospital. I won't be coming out again.

I can breathe, though. They did something to clear my lungs. What happened last night? I can't remember. Jill was near the bed, I started to speak and then everything went black.

I don't feel bad now. Sleepy, far away. They must have given me something for the pain. That's okay.

"Hey, how do you feel?"

It's Sam, trying to smile.

"Okay . . . It's great to breathe again."

"I brought my competition." He puts the tape recorder down near me.

I look at it. My beautiful machine. Did I say anything I wanted to, anything worth saying, anything that will help Jill? If I didn't, then at least I tried. I'm not up to any more.

When I open my eyes again, Sam isn't there. I can't tell if I dozed off or what. Nora is sitting there. "Sam had to go to work," she says.

"Yes, I think he said . . . I can't remember . . . Where's Jill?"

"The lady upstairs said she'd stay with her."

"I worry about her so much!"

"You shouldn't, Kate."

"But will Sam take care of her? I don't want her in an orphanage . . . How can he? He has his work. She's not really his. Why should he be saddled with her for the rest of his life. After all this crud with me. It's enough. When I die, he ought to just walk away."

"If he does, I'll take Jill. If you want me to."

"It's between you and Dr. Gillman . . . But I guess she's too busy."

"I'd raise her right, Kate."

I look at her. Her long, dark hair. That funny smile she has. Then I think of Sam's mother, the other extreme. If you could shake them both up in a bottle, you'd get one person who was just right. "If only Pat was older . . . But I don't know if she'd want a child right now . . . She's not even out of high school."

"What is it about me that bothers you?"

I can't help smiling. "You're messy."

"True."

"You're . . . you slept with Sam."

Her face changes. "Just a couple of times," she says.

"Do you think that was such a crime under the circumstances?"

"Maybe not ... I sound so middle class ... But I want Jill to have stability and order in her life ... You've been good with her, Nora. Thanks."

"I wanted to do it."

It's funny to think that soon I won't be here. I feel fine except for the breathing. I wonder if I said the right thing to Nora. What did I say? "Nora, I—"

But she's not there anymore. I don't remember her leaving. Did I say goodbye to her? Sam is standing near the window. "Will you put the quilt and stuff in a chest? I never got around to it."

"I will."

"And the tapes—"

"I'll have them typed and bound."

"I should have arranged them. You'll never be able to tell which comes where. I'm so damn disorganized."

"No, you're not."

"Dying's such a hassle."

"Don't worry about it ... I'll sort it out."

His face is going away, just slowly. Is he leaving?

"Sam?"

"What, honey?"

"Could you call Dr. Gillman?"

"Kate ... wait."

He begins coming back again. He looks so frightened. "You keep fading away and coming back ... Like some artsy-craftsy movie."

"Dr. Gillman's coming."

"About Jill—"

"I'm going to take care of Jill. What do you think I am?"

"Okay."

"I love her."

"Marry someone . . . who'll be good with her."

"Stop pawning me off on other people . . . I'm married to you."

It's odd. He can't accept it. He's frightened.

Dr. Gillman says, "What do you want for lunch, Kate?"

"A pain pill . . . But don't give me any other drugs to prolong it."

"I won't."

"I want to die on my own clock, all right?"

She nods.

Sam says, "I can't take this, I'm sorry. I—" He runs out.

I look at her. Our eyes meet. "What did I tell you? Mr. Vanishing Act."

"It's hard to watch someone die," Dr. Gillman says. "Maybe harder than it is to die."

Goodbye Sam.

What am I thinking? Not much. About friends and places and dogs I've had. I'm thinking about my little girl, just two, kind of stubby, with golden-blond hair and an attitude toward life that makes me feel small. Thinking about dying and about me and feeling rage that soon there will be no more me. It's hard now. Very hard. I keep thinking, let me wake up just one more morning. There's so much more I have to say to Jill. It's so important.

Goodbye Jill. Jill, my love, my little love. Hang in there, baby.

"Is Sam there?"

"He may be out in the waiting room now. I'll check."

I know he's not there. "Is my mother here?"

"No . . . Would you like me to call her?"

"Stay with me . . . I was going to be brave. But now

... Would you hold my hand?" Dr. Gillman pulls up a chair and takes my hand.

"Is there anything you want to talk about, Kate? Anything you want me to take care of?"

She seems to be so far away, though I can hear her words. I close my eyes, it's easier. I was a virgin when I married David. All the things Mama accused me of ... I loved keeping myself a virgin because she taught me to and I loved her and believed her. Even when she didn't believe me, I went on believing her ... How could she accuse me of being a tramp? I hurt so bad ... I want my mommy to comfort me. "Mama—"

"I'll tell her."

I wonder why Jill is here, why they let her come. I didn't know they allowed children. She looks so nice, playing over there. I don't think she sees me. She's building something with her blocks, some kind of house. The sun looks so pretty on her hair. I always wanted a little girl with blond hair.

On November 10, 1972 Katherine Hayden died in The Niles Clinic in Vancouver. She was twenty years old.